The Kingdom of
What Is

The Kingdom of
What Is

KARL PETERSEN

RESOURCE *Publications* • Eugene, Oregon

THE KINGDOM OF WHAT IS

Resource Publications
An Imprint of Wipf and Stock Publishers
199 W. 8th Ave., Suite 3
Eugene, OR 97401

www.wipfandstock.com

PAPERBACK ISBN: 978-1-5326-1807-9
HARDCOVER ISBN: 978-1-4982-4331-5
EBOOK ISBN: 978-1-4982-4330-8

Manufactured in the U.S.A.   MAY 18, 2017 *for Kaitlyn and Karis*

Contents

The Palace

Downsfield River

The Darklands

River Royal

Ocean

Gulls Landing

Whale Back Rock

Batty Woods

Fisherman's Cove

Dead Man's Creek

The Kingdom of What Is

Downsfield

The Great Gorge

Bounty Downs

The Farms

The Caves

Grover + Aster

Singing Meadow

Budsley Pond

Rocky Mound

Wild Rose Passage

Shelby

school

park

home

Chapter 1

A Passage

Everyone had left the lunch room for their afternoon classes, except for Kate and a couple stragglers. Kate sat leaning on her elbow and poking unconsciously at a baggie of celery sticks on the lunch table. She whirled in her chair when she heard her friend Analyse call.

"Wake up, Kate! The bell!"

Kate swept her uneaten lunch items off the table into her bag, jumped up, and trotted down the hall through the gauntlet of lockers to Ms. Lee's English class. She plunked herself down in a seat next to Analyse.

"What's wrong?" Analyse said. "Your eyes are all red."

Kate hadn't been sleeping well. She knew she looked horrible, and she hadn't bothered trying to make herself look any better than she felt. She stared at her desk, letting her tangle of brown hair drape over her face. Her purple hair streaks hung in unkempt strands. She looked through her veil of hair at Ms. Lee standing at the front of the class. She was explaining their next writing exercise, but her voice was a distant drone.

"Kate? Any problems?" Ms. Lee was asking.

Kate heard her name in a tunnel. She looked up, dazed. Yeah, she thought, problems, but not for sharing. She heard people snickering and whispering.

"Hey, Zombie . . . It's not Halloween yet . . . She must be on drugs." The voices echoed.

The boy sitting across from her was making ghost noises. "Hi, spooky. Your hair's as crazy as mine, look." He shook his head to make his long locks cover his face. Several other kids laughed.

Analyse grabbed the boy by the ear and held on until he squealed. "Nobody's as crazy as you, Cody," she hissed in his ear. "You're gonna fail grade eight again."

No, Kate would not lash out, even at despicable Cody. She would not give anyone the satisfaction of seeing her cry. She was used to being "weird," and she didn't care what they thought. She picked up her backpack, walked up to Ms. Lee, and told her she wasn't feeling well and had to go home.

Before she left the room, she turned and faced her classmates defiantly. She wanted them to see her as she was—red eyes, disheveled hair, and all. And she wanted them to know she was not ashamed or defeated by their mocking.

It wasn't until she got out into the hall that her eyes welled up. She wiped her face and went into the office to tell the secretary she needed to go home. Principal Brodeur's habitual sniffing could be heard coming from his adjoining office. The secretary said she'd call home for Kate, but before she could finish dialing, Kate had gone, the front door of school swinging shut behind her. Her mom would not be surprised to see her.

Home was only two blocks away, but before she reached there, she stopped at the park and found her favorite thinking spot in a plum tree near the play area. She and her younger brother Gavin called this tree the poop tree because of the galls growing around the limbs, which looked remarkably like dog poop on a skewer. The tree was diseased and hadn't grown plums for a couple of years, but it had a prime sitting nook that Kate liked. She leaned over a branch chest high and let her feet dangle below. With the help of her long hair locks and willowy limbs, she blended perfectly with the tree and disappeared. She glanced around at the growing number of galls on the branches *sans* plums.

"Hi poop kebabs," she said casually.

She glanced across the street to her house. Her mom would have got the call from school by now and would be unsurprised. And she would probably guess she was in the park if she didn't show up right away. Kate needed some time by herself. She told herself that when her dad came back home, everything would be fine. She spotted Gavin playing in front of their house. That morning he'd said he didn't want to go to school, and with the situation at home, Mom didn't argue.

Kate looked to the far side of the park. A large wooded area lay just across the street that marked the end of the park, which was also the town limits of Shelby. She had been to those woods many times with her family, walking the well-groomed trails. Her family called it "Time Out Woods" because they used it for a time out when someone got upset or just needed a change of scenery. It was the cure to anything negative. If her dad were here, that's where she'd want to be right now, walking the trails with him.

She knew her dad at his happiest when he was in those woods, and simply thinking about being there with him made her feel a little better. Because of him, Kate grew to love the woods. She often thought he should have been a science teacher rather than a history prof. As a toddler, she would listen to him telling her the names of the various trees and birds. Soon she could distinguish robins and wrens and thrushes by their trills. He told her how to identify certain woodpeckers by the kinds of holes they left in trees.

A stream ran through the center of the woods beneath large sweeping maples. They watched salmon spawn there as the tireless fish flipped and flopped upstream to lay eggs. The sight of them the first time gave Kate the creeps—their scarred, torn bodies with patches of flesh entirely missing.

"Yuck, they're a mess!" she said.

"Sure, from their long fight upstream from the sea," her dad said. "They give everything they've got for their future young and then they die."

"That's sad. Don't talk about that."

But her dad said to think about how courageous they were. "The same story is whispered and repeated everywhere you look. Life, love, death, and new life again—a cycle. We have to respect that or we lose it. The first rule of the woods—respect."

Her dad was old-fashioned in a cool sort of way.

And one time years ago, he showed Kate a sad story of the woods—a place that had once been a beaver pond. He told her wistfully about the life that had been there before people turned the pond into a place to dump old car tires, bottles, rusted bikes, skateboards, and headless dolls. The surface of the water was covered in an oily sheen.

Sitting in the poop tree now, Kate recalled the way things were with her dad at home, the way things should always be.

Time Out Woods lay hiding behind a dreary October mist, as if it understood her. Crows squabbled over brimming garbage cans nearby like a family fighting over the last piece of cake. In the distance Kate heard the ice cream truck making the rounds and stirring up the few toddlers in the playground with its familiar tune.

When she was a toddler, Kate eventually discovered kids were getting delicious looking stuff from that truck and that it didn't just play tunes. The driver always had to yell at the kids to move back, but she ignored him one day and poked her head through the open door to see what hidden treasures lay beyond the music.

She reached in her lunch for the sandwich she had not eaten at school. As she took a bite, she heard a low croaking sound behind her. She craned her neck to find a crow perched in a branch just above her head. She looked more closely. The crow had a white wing feather that stuck out ever so slightly. "How did you get that white feather?" she asked, musing to herself. "Like a hair streak. Wow, cool crow!"

She also noticed a piece of paper in its beak. The crow cocked its head as if to examine Kate's face before it dropped the paper, letting it flutter down into Kate's lap. It was a photo of Kate's family, together, sitting on the front steps of the house. In the picture they are all in shorts and T-shirts. She and her brother are sitting one step down in front of their parents. Her mom's hair is pulled back in a pony, and her dad still has his beard. He has his arm around her mom's shoulder, and they are all genuinely smiling.

That was before it blew up and all went to pieces.

Kate turned to the crow. "Hey, where did you get—?"

But the crow flew off before she could finish, its white feather flashing like a sliver of sunlight breaking through the mist. It landed in another tree, looked back at Kate, and croaked. She jumped down and ran to it. As she came near, the crow flew off and landed again, going from tree to tree until Kate had followed it all the way to the far side of the park. She crossed the street that marked the boundary of Shelby and stood before a hedge of wild roses at the edge of Time Out Woods.

A strange, warm breeze was blowing from the woods, and Kate caught a whiff of strawberries. Strawberries? But it was October. Strawberry season had long passed. There was another gust of wind, warmer this time, and the smell was stronger. She dropped her backpack at the rose hedge and parted the bushes, careful to avoid the thorns. She looked beyond into a small clearing dappled with sunlight. This was odd, Kate thought, because behind her the park was still shrouded in a cold, light rain.

The usual entrance to the woods, which had a marked path beginning at the street, was about a hundred feet from where she stood. But rather than take that, she chose instead to push through the rose bushes toward the small area of light and the smell of strawberries. She crawled, thorns scratching and snagging on the back of her hoodie.

She finally came through and found herself standing ankle deep in a patch of strawberries. She picked one, tasted it, and then popped it into the back of her mouth. A burst of energy rushed through her, and her senses came alive. Every smell of the woods seemed to rush to her nose at once. The colors in the woods became sharper and more distinct than she had ever seen them before, and the breeze seemed to go down into the roots of her hair.

It was like summer in the middle of October! It was so warm she removed her hoodie. Blossoms covered the rose bushes, and the trees were leafy green, while outside in Shelby the trees were losing their leaves in the chill of fall.

"So you decided to come after all," said a voice.

Kate looked up startled. Above her in an old broad maple sat the crow with the white wing feather. Kate darted back toward the rose briars.

"Kind of silly to run back now after all that fighting through the rose hedge," the bird called after her.

"Uh . . . " Kate stuttered. "I was just following . . . you. I thought . . . you wanted me to."

"I was hoping, but I expected you'd shrug it off like everyone else. Why did you come?"

"I . . . I was bored, I guess. Doldrums?" Kate said.

"Doldrums. Others have ventured into the Kingdom because of doldrums. But I don't think that's why you came."

"The kingdom?"

"Yes."

"Kingdom of what?" Kate asked.

"Of what?" echoed the crow, cocking its head to one side.

"You said *the kingdom*. The kingdom of what . . . or who?"

"The Kingdom of What or Who? Never heard of it."

"No, the kingdom of, like, you know . . . who?"

The crow shifted on its branch. "Never heard of the Kingdom of Like You Know Who either."

"I mean what do you call . . . this kingdom? The kingdom of who? Who?"

The crow cocked its head again and squawked. "The Kingdom of Hoo Hoo? We do have owls . . . but it's not only theirs. It's everybody's . . . and everything's."

"What?" asked Kate.

"Neither the Kingdom of What nor Hoo. It's simply the Kingdom."

"The Kingdom?"

"That's it, you've got it. I know, in your world, you like to give the Kingdom names, like New York, or England, or Shelby, or Kathmandu . . . But here it's just the Kingdom of . . . of what is."

"The Kingdom of What Is?"

The crow cackled a long laugh."Well, if you must give it a name, the Kingdom of What Is is as fine and fitting as any."

Kate suddenly shivered at the thought of talking to a crow.

"Oh acorns, I'm scaring you, aren't I?"

"Sort of, yeah. Where did you get this picture?" she asked, holding up the photo.

"I was rummaging through the garbage in the alley and I recognized you, saw you sitting in the plum tree, and the rest, as they say, is your history."

"My history, yes. We're not like this anymore . . . I mean, like, together. My dad left."

"I'm very sorry," the crow said in a tone that sounded more genuinely sympathetic than any voice she'd heard for quite some time.

There was a long pause. "Me and my dad, we came to these woods a lot, but today it's not at all the same. It's, like, enchanted. And you, you're—"

"If you mean 'enchanted' as in fairies and pixie dust, I'm afraid you'll be disappointed. You won't find any dragons, ogres, gnomes, or unicorns and the like here. They've been rumored to exist, but none found."

Of course not, Kate thought. Nothing as silly as a talking crow, and then blurted, "But none of this is real!"

"If you're here long enough, you'll find the Kingdom may be more real than what you're used to." The crow sighed deeply and looked off into the distance, as if he was taken by the simple wonder of the place himself. Then he cleared his throat and unfolded his wings as if to fly.

"Wait! Wait!" Kate said. "How . . . "

The crow relaxed. "Yes, how," he said and preened his white wing feather, thinking for a moment. "You want to know how you got here. Well, some would say that you brought yourself, but that would be ignoring that, mostly, you were *drawn* here, quite beside yourself."

"Drawn here?"

"You couldn't resist, right? You're a sensitive one, for sure. Others catch sight of this, through the trees, several times over several years, but miss it and never come in. But you, you've fallen right in, more or less beside yourself."

"Beside myself," Kate repeated to herself.

"Yes, with delight . . . wonder . . . curiosity. Some have found their way in by hacking through the underbrush until they find that they are indeed in. Whatever their reasons, they eventually realize they were actually drawn in and have come running, fighting, or more often falling in unwittingly."

"Unwitt . . . what?"

"Unsuspectingly . . . without knowing it . . . by surprise . . . quite beside themselves. Like you. Some have likened it to 'falling in love.' But falling into the Kingdom is much more profound and more lasting." The crow scraped its beak on the tree limb. "Sorry for all the primping," he said. "There's only so much I can take of the garbage you've got out there in those barrels. Eventually, it just sticks to your beak like a bad grub. Anyway . . . how you got here, yes. It's like hearing a tune a few times, and before you know it, you find yourself humming it to yourself. And you'll hum it over and over until, eventually, the tune becomes a part of you."

"Like an ice cream truck tune," Kate said. "And after the tune, the ice cream becomes a part of you, right?" She chuckled to herself.

"Wait . . . did you say ice cream?"

Kate was caught off guard. "Yes, why? You eat ice cream?"

"The occasional drip or two, if I'm lucky. You don't have any, do you?"

"Uh, no, not . . . "

"Never mind. I'll have to do some scouting. To your point, like the tune from an ice cream truck, I suppose, if you consider that kind of tune catchy. But I suspect you like the tune because it comes with the ice cream, right?"

"Yeah, of course."

"Fair enough. A tune is only as good as its reward."

The crow raised one wing tip, beckoning Kate to follow deeper into the woods. She hesitated, her heart pounding. Every tree, every quickening scent and warm ray of sunlight told her to keep going. But following crows was ridiculous, she told herself, and talking with them was plain loony. And her mom would be wondering where she was by now. She pushed her way back through the rose briars. She was halfway when a branch snagged on her hoodie. She pulled, but the rose branch hung to her stubbornly like a long slender arm that would not let her go.

Chapter 2

Wild Goose Chase

After Kate finally pulled herself loose from the thorns, she peeked through the rose hedge toward home. Leaves were falling, and the mist was still hanging over the park, hemming things in and making Shelby feel even smaller and more depressing than it already was. She would not go back, not yet.

She turned back around to where she'd left the crow. It was gone. She took a couple deep breaths. The pure air seemed to lift her off her feet. Then she noticed—she wasn't feeling tired any more.

There was the sound of splashing from deeper in the woods. Kate took a few steps down a path she recognized. There was another splash. She came to a pond she knew as Burton Pond, yet it was not Burton Pond. This was larger and cleaner, with no car tires, toys, and tin cans.

She heard something like a creaking wood gate, and out of the corner of her eye saw something falling. She jumped instinctively as a tree crashed down into the water just ten feet away. In seconds two beavers were sliding into the water and working furiously on the branches. One of them came directly toward Kate with a limb in its mouth. The beaver dropped the branch and looked her in the eye, opening and closing its mouth as if gnawing at thin air.

Kate's breath caught in her throat. Was this beaver trying to speak to her? She first heard clicks and static, like a radio tuning to find a station. The beaver continued mouthing at her until she thought she heard, "This is mine."

The beaver climbed to where Kate stood and prodded her foot with its nose. She jumped back. Then she heard it again, still somewhat fuzzy. "Do you mind, we're working here." The beaver busily poked the branch into an interlocking system of twigs. The beaver seemed to be half singing and half whistling to itself. Kate leaned in closer to listen.

"Hither, thither, under and yon. On and on we go," the beaver repeated.

"*You* talk too? " Kate said, her heart pounding.

"And whistle," the beaver said.

"What?" Kate pulled her hair back to hear better.

"I try not to talk much, try to work more."

Kate, at a loss, absent mindedly picked up a branch, as the beaver was doing, and tried to push it into place.

"No, no! Just leave it lie," the beaver barked. This she heard clearly. "Why do you people always think you know better how to do things? We're trying to keep up here, and to this point we've done quite well doing it our way, thank you very much."

Kate now saw that she had been standing at the end of a dam that extended along one end of the pond. The beaver grunted and poked.

"Oh, fudittle dum," it muttered. "Second thought, now that you're here, hand me that twig by your foot there." Kate did so and stepped back while the beaver plied the twig into place. "That'll do. Terrific wind these last few days and then a freak rain storm, downpour, broke the dam. We're only now sorting it out. Something's gone amiss."

"Is this Burton Pond?" Kate asked.

"Burton? No Burton around here, and if there was, he shouldn't have the brass to name a pond after himself. This one, like everything else here, is royal land. We work hard to keep it in good shape, but that doesn't mean we go naming things after ourselves. Where you off to? A jaunt to the meadow? Tour of the castle? Off you go then. Say hello to the King and Queen, and tell them we would be much obliged if they could do something about the gunk coming in here from upstream. Don't know how long we can hold on."

Kate glanced over to where a small stream emptied into the far end of the pond and asked, "Did you say castle? Where?"

"No idea," said the beaver, jostling another branch into place. "Somewhere in the center of things."

"Where's the center of things?" Kate asked.

The beaver paused, as though he'd never consider the question himself. "Neither here nor there. Betwixt and between near and nether, I suppose."

"I see," said Kate though she obviously didn't.

"Sensible creatures don't go around asking such questions. They just accept it and live by it."

Kate persisted. "But you said the center of things. If you don't know where it is, how do you know if it . . . ? Wait, the center of *what* things?"

"Center of the Kingdom, of course." The beaver cast her a quizzical eye as if Kate must be from another world not to know the answer to her question.

"How far is the center from here?"

"Far and away. But if you really insist, you should ask one of the crows or deer. Never been there myself."

"Then how do you know there *is* a castle? And a king and queen?"

"Oh, they're there. I trust the ones who've been there and seen it. We beavers have got no time for a trip of that distance. I tend to my work and live happily—take care of the family, have a drink after work with my buddies, and sing to the moon when the spirit moves me."

He continued moving feverishly to repair the dam. Kate saw something flash over the pond and then heard the rattling of a kingfisher, which landed on a beaver lodge.

"You say you 'live happily' in this beautiful place," Kate commented, "but you don't seem happy."

"Okay, I'm fair to middling if you want the truth," the beaver admitted. "Was feeling better before all this started." The beaver cursed, jabbing another branch into place. "The water's fouled, weather's out of whack, animals are dying, humans are disappearing, and no one seems to care." He looked up at Kate. "But we would be well served if someone, say someone with strong, young legs . . . could get a message to the palace for us while we slave out here in the nether regions of the Kingdom . . . someone, for instance, who can cover a vast distance faster than a beaver." The beaver held its gaze.

Kate could feel the beaver's helplessness. "What kind of message do you want sent?"

"How about starting with a message about the mess? They can take it from there. We're not the one's pulling the strings here, we're just trying to hold up our end."

"Is that the stream you're talking about?" Kate pointed to the far end of the pond.

"Truly," said the beaver, without looking up, and slipped back into the water.

Kate was curious about the gunk and followed the trail along the pond toward the far end. From there she continued up a trail along the stream, then stopped when she saw a dark inky line in the water weaving downstream. She broke off a small leafy branch, knelt down close to the stream, and stuck it into the water. The black inky substance thickened and swirled around the branch like a snake coiling around its prey. She felt a downward sucking motion and quickly drew the stick back. The branch was covered with the black gunk. She was about to touch it when she saw the leaves of the branch she held wither before her eyes and fall to the ground.

She scrambled back to the trail. She knew not far up the stream was a fence that marked the boundary of Time Out Woods and beyond was a farmer's field. She followed the path, which came not to a fence but to a large open meadow. Hills rose gradually on either side, covered in patches of wild flowers that shimmered in the breeze like a hologram in hues of green, lavender and orange. The stream ran through this meadow to the beaver pond. The colorful meadow wrapped around her feet—a lush, billowy quilt. Kate was overcome with a happiness she had not felt for a very long time, if ever, and wanted to scream. So she did, and followed that with a loud laugh.

At the crest of the hill to her right, Kate noticed an orange glow rising. A fire? The glow seemed to pulse every few seconds, growing stronger and then weaker in intensity. As she watched, from her left a flock of geese came gliding toward her, looking as though they would land. Their honking grew louder. About twenty geese descended with their wings spread, landing in a cascade of honking and a flurry of wings that blew her hair. She stepped back as a musty, wild odour from the geese wafted over her.

"We are here, one and all," one honked, "at your beckoning call."

Kate stood spellbound at the throng of chattering geese, or at least she thought she was hearing chatter.

"A young waif with mouth agape," they honked, "but no call at all. We heard a scream, and a girl's laugh. If not you, was it another lass?"

"No, that was me, but—"

A loud chorus rose from the geese.

"We not only fly but sing too, so what can we do for you?"

"Uhm, I'm not sure."

The geese suddenly became very still, befuddled that Kate seemed to have no plan.

"A human without direction. Tsk, tsk, 'tis a dereliction."

"Do you have to talk in rhymes?"

"Very well, everyone, as she wishes. No more rhyming flourishes. Ach! Forgive the rhyming, it's vital for timing. Can't lose the practice of rhythm and rhyme. All could be lost without flying in time," rhymed the goose as if it couldn't help itself.

"Could you stop the rapping for a second?"

The geese all jerked their heads left and right. "Rap, rap, rap," they echoed quizzically to one another. Twenty necks formed question marks in the air.

The one goose that seemed to be the leader of the flock finally suggested, "Shall we simply say . . . hop aboard?"

Kate looked at them completely confused. "Hop aboard?"

"A couple of us, take your pick now without fuss. For our information, where's your destination?"

"I don't know," Kate said.

"Okay, let's see, where would you most *like* to be?"

"The palace?" Kate said, more as a question than a request, since she wasn't even sure there was a palace.

The gaggle turned their heads to one another, repeating "palace . . . palace . . . palace."

The lead goose spoke. "However, I would not advise going to the palace unless you're on serious business with the King or Queen. Tourists have gone and left again disjointed and disappointed." The gaggle's voices rose in confirmation.

"I'm not . . . I am not a tourist," Kate said emphatically, surprising herself. "I'm on business. For the beavers. I need to see the King."

"The King and Queen! King and Queen!" they repeated in a crescendo.

"To the palace, for the beavers! We're high achievers!" the lead goose announced.

It then bowed its head low in the grass at Kate's feet and spread its wings wide while another goose did the same immediately behind the first. Kate was assisted in lying face down across the backs of the two crouching geese so that her chest was on the front goose and her feet rested on the back of the trailing goose.

Kate was instructed to wrap her hands around the breast of the front goose but *not* to grab its neck, which could cut off the goose's voice and breathing, making flying much more difficult than it had to be. After she got over the ticklish sensation on her stomach from the feathers, Kate could relax. One goose explained there was a tricky maneuver she would have to perform for landing, but they would cross that bridge when they came to it.

"Trust us, trust us, trust us!" The chorus rose, as they lifted off the ground flapping furiously. Kate was shocked how flapping wings could be so deafening. They rose above the meadow in a crooked but purposeful V. A strange but profound calm came over her. With her cheek against the back of the lead goose, she was lost in the steady rhythm of wings.

In a few minutes, they came over a range of hills into a spacious valley with a wide river and several villages. The surrounding slopes were carpeted by a thatch work of vineyards, pastures, and farms, ending at the edge of forests in the upper regions.

"There she be!" called the lead goose breaking the way.

Kate looked down. "Where?" she asked.

"Right there, along the River Royal. Among the gardens and the wine-rich soil."

Kate saw orchards and gardens but no palace. Then she saw it—a collection of buildings, mostly squat and randomly arranged, surrounded by a wall that had several gaps. There was one building larger than the others in the center of the compound. But none of this looked so impressive as to be called a palace.

As her carriers descended, a closer view disclosed castle walls in a state of disrepair and weathered by the years. Parts of the walls were broken out, leaving piles of rubble where they had crumbled. There was nothing about it that resembled a fortified castle for a king or queen who would rule such an exceptional kingdom as this. There were towers, or their remnants, at several places along the wall. She did not notice any canons anywhere as you might expect. In fact, there was nothing royal about this palace. Except for its very large size, it was unremarkable and could easily be overlooked as nothing but old ruins.

Perhaps it had been overrun and was being looted because Kate could now see people moving in and out through a large opening in the wall. Or perhaps these were tourists. Some people appeared to be floating along the ground like ghosts though the angle of the sun may have been playing tricks on her.

"That's the castle?" Kate asked, defeated. There was no response except for an outburst of song from the throng of geese, as confident and heartfelt as you could want, as they slowed to a gliding descent.

Come in, come in to the royal courts,

riding, walking, day and night.
Strangers and kin, strong and fallen,
draw near the halls of burden and light.

At the word "fallen," Kate remembered that she was suspended hundreds of feet in the air on a pair of geese. And she was descending on this scene of strange royalty attended by ghosts! Suddenly it all felt to her like a trick—complete nonsense. She doubted any real palace lay below at all. Regret filled her.

"No, don't land! Don't land!" she shouted. "Turn back!"

Her able entourage obediently veered off their landing course and wheeled around toward the meadow, back to where they had started. When they finally descended to the plush, flowered field, just five feet above the ground the trailing goose let Kate's feet fall free.

The lead goose shouted, "Hang on until your feet touch the ground."

Kate clung to her lone carrier. It flapped vigorously just above the ground so that Kate's feet came to rest softly in the grass. She had barely turned to apologize to her gracious company for her indecisive behavior before they rose again in a chorus of honking. With a vague wave of her hand she watched them go.

Kate regretted leaving her half-eaten lunch at the rose hedge. Hunger, she realized, was as real here in this Kingdom of What Is as it was at home. At least there was plenty of water. She knelt down by a rivulet that trickled from the hills into the meadow. It appeared clear and clean. She cupped her hands and dipped them in and was rewarded with the most refreshing, mildly sweet water she'd ever had. It seemed not only her thirst was satisfied, but her hunger passed as well.

With the warmth of the goose still clinging to her chest, Kate suddenly realized she'd entered the woods more than an hour ago. She felt for her watch and remembered she had left it in her backpack. She walked quickly, trying to think of an explanation for where she'd been that would satisfy her mom.

Once outside the wild rose hedge, she grabbed her pack and raced across the park, a thick carpet of leaves squishing beneath her feet. Rain splattered her face. She rushed through the front door, apologizing as she caught her breath.

"Sorry I'm so late, Mom! I stopped in the park for a bit, and I guess I just lost track of time. Did the office call?"

"Yes, they called a minute ago. Come here and tell me what's up. You're looking a bit pale. How did you get that scratch on your cheek?"

Kate's hand went to her cheek. She'd been scratched going through the rose briars.

"And what do you mean 'so late'?" her mom asked.

Kate glanced at the kitchen clock. It read 1:45. How could that be? She had left school at 1:30, sat in the park, and then gone into the woods for more than an hour.

Chapter 3

No Help

Tree limbs whipped back and forth outside Kate's bedroom, and rain blew against the window. Just as well. She was in bed sick and had thrown up more times than she wanted to count. She figured it had to be the mysterious black gunk—there must have been some in the water she drank at the meadow.

She was too tired to do anything but lie in bed and slept until she didn't know what time or day it was. When she could finally move around, she found out she'd slept through a whole day and missed school. Her mom offered her some soup, but the thought of eating only made her feel nauseous. She went back to bed and lay staring at the ceiling. In spite of getting so sick, she could not stop thinking about Time Out Woods—the crow, the beaver, that amazing ride on the geese! Was it real? Maybe she had been feeling so down that she was hallucinating.

It was only three weeks ago that her mom and dad had their big explosion, ending with her dad walking out the door with nothing but the one thing he was never separated from, his briefcase—one of the old flexible leather kind, handed down to him by his father. Kate's mom said he held on to it like old expectations that wouldn't let go.

Before getting into the car that day, visibly broken, her dad had turned to Kate. "I'll be back," he said, choking back tears and giving her a brief hug. He did come back when no one was around, they noticed, because his clothes and his personal things were gone. The light that was normally the beacon in their house had gone out for Kate.

After that day, her sadness like a thick cloud had blown in over everything, coming and going in waves without warning. In the moments when

Kate was feeling a little better, she knew the cloud was only waiting outside to come blowing back in.

Her mom never gave her a straight answer about why her dad had left, just that they were "having problems." Other than that, there was only silence—a void between Kate and her mom that could not be crossed. Her mom tried to ease the anguish by telling Kate she could still meet her dad for lunch and talk with him on the phone, but Kate told her that was hardly the same as having him at home.

He did phone and talked with Kate about everything except about when he was coming home, which was what she really wanted to hear. And, like Mom, he said nothing about what had happened between them. "We just have to work out a few problems," he'd say and then change the subject to school or gymnastics. It was the line they agreed on, one they'd obviously rehearsed—"working out some problems." It was their Big Secret, and she was not allowed in on it. She was beginning to doubt he would ever come home.

The next day was Saturday. Kate and Gavin's godparents, Dennis and Jackie, were visiting for dinner. Her mom hoped that maybe these long-time friends could lift their spirits. Dennis and Jackie adored the kids. But to Kate the chatter over dinner was simply people trying to put a cheerful face on everything that was crappy, like music at Walmart. She picked quietly at her spaghetti and let her mind wander elsewhere.

"Kate came down with something the other day, so her appetite isn't quite there yet," her mom explained.

But her stomach was not the problem. For one thing, she couldn't stop thinking about her visit to Time Out Woods, which was still as vivid in her mind as the scratches on her cheek. She really had felt "beside herself," as the crow said, as if it were all happening to someone else, and she was just there watching beside herself in complete wonder. But how could she simply have made it all up?

"Kate. Kate?" Her mom tapped her on the arm. "Jackie asked you something."

"Sorry. I guess I'm still out of it, my stomach . . . "

The visit of her godparents, spaghetti dinner—it did nothing to cheer up the evening. One important ingredient was missing—the person normally in the empty chair at the end of the table. If her dad were there, Kate knew, there would be genuine laughter and happy feelings. He could bring life to any situation. Now there were only forced murmurs and clinking forks and knives.

Kate felt a tear come to her eye and quickly wiped it away. It was like a play where she could only sit and watch the set being adjusted and actors murmuring back stage. But the Big Secret just hung there like a curtain that never opened.

Jackie tried to make conversation. "So how's grade eight, Kate?"

Kate and Gavin were at different schools right across the street from each other, Gavin in grade five at Shelby Elementary and Kate in grade eight at Shelby High, only five minutes from home.

"Ms. Lee's pretty cool," Kate finally offered. "She's letting us listen to an audio book of *Hamlet*."

"Wow, how do you like that?"

"Mm, I don't know . . . kind of hard. I guess you could say they have a few problems to work out." Kate's mom stopped in mid-bite, and Kate caught her eye.

"My, Shakespeare," Dennis said. "No more kid's stuff, right?" He leaned over to Kate."You'll pull it off."

Kate had to admit there were some things about grade eight she liked. Ms. Lee was finally a teacher she could relate to, a bit quirky, like herself. She treated them like grownups. And there was this guy in her class, Nolan, who liked her even though she was a bit off, but she didn't know if she liked him yet. The best thing was she'd be turning thirteen soon, which meant her mom wouldn't be interfering as much.

Gavin interjected, trying to be part of the conversation. "The other day a boy in my class stole somebody's chicken nuggets from their lunch and ate 'em and then just laughed, and he never got punished or anything for it. It sucks."

"Now Mom, remember that," Kate said. "The next time he goes sneaking into my room without my permission and takes something, he should get punished, right Gavin? I want my privacy, got it?"

Since their dad left, Gavin had been "acting out more," as their mom put it. He'd been getting into his sister's stuff, scrawling pictures of monsters and war, and taping them all over the house.

"Do you guys ever go to Time Out Woods?" Kate suddenly asked Dennis and Jackie.

"It's what we call the woods across the park," her mom explained.

"No, is it nice?" Jackie asked.

"We go there with Dad sometimes," Gavin said, "after he and Mom have a fight." Jackie put her napkin to her mouth as if she'd said it herself and was pushing the comment back into her mouth.

"Or it's a good place to go if we just need a place to unwind," Mom added.

"And talk with the crows," Kate added with a smile, searching their faces for a reaction.

Everyone laughed. Kate's comment had broken the tension. Dennis agreed that crows actually do sound like people talking sometimes. And this set off a string of stories about the times they'd felt crows were "talking" to them.

Mom said, "When they start screaming at each other right outside the bedroom at six in the morning, I let Norbert out, and he goes right up the tree after them."

"Yeah," Gavin said, "I heard one crow say, 'Ach, ach, this cat is driving me nuts!'"

Again, there was laughter from everyone but Kate. If she had said what she was thinking, like "No, crows really do talk, and they're pretty smart, and they love ice cream, and I'd like you to meet one," they would have thought she needed a shrink.

The next day, Kate, Gavin and their mom were picking up the branches that had been knocked down by the storm, and Kate was wondering about when she could get back to Time Out Woods and how she could get there without her mom or Gavin knowing.

Suddenly, she announced, "Hey, let's go for a walk in Time Out Woods. It's Sunday."

Her mom looked up and brushed the hair from her face, grateful Kate was cheering up and was interested in doing something fun.

"Why not, let's go," her mom said, taking off her gloves. "I'll call Dennis and Jackie."

A few minutes later Dennis arrived without Jackie, who was too busy.

Kate knew that if they could see for themselves what she had experienced, she could be sure she was not nuts. They entered the woods as they usually did, via the marked trail that started from the street bordering the park. Only a few feet into the woods, the trail split in two directions. A sign indicated "Burton Pond, 200 meters" and "Rocky Mound, 1 km" to the left. The other way to the right was "Miners Gulch, 5 km." Kate and her family knew these places well.

As they walked toward Burton Pond, Kate wondered if they would meet the beaver and if they would be greeted by the same mysterious warmth and fragrance of the woods. They neared the spot where she had met the crow, and Kate let the others go ahead.

Nothing was as it had been. Time Out Woods was as she'd always known it. The chilly fall air that was outside was in the woods also. She noticed no rare, sweet aroma, and there were no strawberries out of season. In a dead tree, several crows perched motionless like dots on a dot-to-dot puzzle waiting to be drawn in. She scanned the crowd for a white feather. One squawked weakly, but none were talking. She called out, "Hey, I'm back! White-feather crow!" and felt stupid when there was no answer. She ran to catch up to the others.

They passed at Burton Pond, still filthy, and stopped on Rocky Mound, a small hill with several large sitting rocks at its top that looked down to where the meadow she'd discovered should have been but where there was now simply woods.

"What were you yelling at back there?" Kate's mom asked.

"Oh nothing, just felt like yelling, sort of."

From Rocky Mound they could see a fence that marked the boundary of Time Out Woods. Beyond the fence were farmers' fields. Mom and Dennis sat next to each other a little further down the hill, talking intently.

Kate remembered the last time she'd been at this spot with her family, with her dad there. To the left had stood Mom with her arms folded, and at a distance to the right stood Dad with his hands in his pockets. The whole time, they never glanced at each other or said a word. It had hurt Kate to see them so alone and so distant from each other then.

Kate could overhear her mom say to Dennis, "She's depressed, she's missing her dad." Dennis put his arm around her mom's shoulder and pulled her close. She rested her head on his shoulder. Soon they stood up. It was time to go.

As the day passed, Kate was ready to let her strange visit to Time Out Woods pass, probably a momentary fantasy. But then Monday morning in class, something Ms. Lee said caused the woods to come knocking on the door in Kate's brain again.

"Our imaginations are vital because they tell us what is most important to us, what we fear, and what we want to be true," Ms. Lee said. "With our imaginations we create dreams. But we should take the next step. We need to pursue our dreams until they come true." She asked them to write a paragraph about something that was not true that they wanted to be true.

Kate wrote two paragraphs, then three and four, about a land where animals talked, where strawberries grew lush and wild, and where people could fly. Then she quickly crumpled her paper and stuffed it into her backpack.

The pressure was building. If her discovery was real, she should not keep it to herself. At the same time, she could not share it with just anyone. If everyone heard about it, Time Out Woods would easily be overrun by people who did not share the same seriousness she felt. And the authorities would probably shut it down.

After school, Nolan ran past her down the hall. He waved as he passed and said, "Hey, talk to ya later," and raced off after a few guys with a football, his lanky legs twirling beneath him like an egg beater. He was a bit clumsy, but that's why Kate liked him. He was a good guy, accepting of her weirdness. If she told him about the Kingdom of What Is, he'd probably just say "wow, cool."

Kate sat at the side of the athletic field with Analyse. The girls were first drawn to each other a year ago because they were natural loners, and loners always seemed to end up finding each other. Kate's quiet nature was often mistaken for weakness, but Analyse knew Kate was anything but weak. Analyse loved her inner resolve. Other than her dad, Kate trusted Analyse more than anyone.

Kate pulled at a few blades of grass, looked across the athletic field, and finally confided in Analyse, who was the class brainiac and always had something smart or interesting to say. And she was blunt, so Kate knew she would say what she thought.

"So," she asked Kate, "they had a big fight and your dad just left?"

"Something like that."

"Well, if it helps at all, my mom and dad split up a few times and always came back together again. Adults are just fickle."

"First Dad leaves, and then this thing in the woods happened," Kate said. She told her about the strange warmth and the uncommonly clean air, the beauty of the place, and also about the dark gunk in the stream. She didn't say anything about the goose ride or talking animals. She thought a little at a time would be best. She didn't want to completely turn her off.

Analyse looked out over the athletic field and pushed up on the bridge of her wire-rimmed glasses. "So maybe the two are linked, like twin events," she offered. "Your dad leaves, and then the thing in the woods. Strange things happen in pairs. Like you and me."

They laughed, and the boys out on the football field glanced their way, thinking the girls were laughing at them. Two teams were in a scuffle over the football with Nolan on the bottom, clawing like a cat with all fours at a grade nine boy.

"Why do boys have to act so weird when there's a ball involved?" Analyse wondered. "Forget about Nolan, okay, he's just into football. Plus, he's kinda dorky."

"If I didn't like dorks, you wouldn't be my friend," Kate said.

"Very funny. But to be fair, I'm not a dork, I'm a nerd," Analyse clarified.

"I told you, Nolan and me, we're just friends. It's not like special or anything."

"Okay. Sorry."

"Lyse, I know you're going to think I'm crazy, but I have to tell you something else . . . about the woods." Kate told her about the crow, the beavers, and the rapping geese. Analyse listened patiently, wrinkling her nose a couple of times, while pulling at loose ends in her long curly red hair.

Analyse asked, "Have you been reading kids' books, Kate? Crows may sound like they're talking, but it's not real. You know that, right? Maybe you just heard 'babble, babble, babble' and it came out like words and you turned it into sentences. And riding on the backs of geese? Come on."

"But it was different. I've been feeling butterflies in my stomach ever since, I can't stop thinking about it."

Analyse pushed her hair back over her shoulder. "Well, I guess I felt something like that when Jeremy held hands with me this summer. But then I found out he held Tamilya Walker's hand, too, and then everything just went back to ordinary again."

"Yeah, but I'm not talking about anything like a crush," Kate said.

Analyse suggested, "Maybe somebody's putting a spell on you . . . you know, sorcery."

"You don't mean like a witch's spell, do you?"

"It has to be. That stuff about talking animals and unusual smells only happens when someone's playing around with magic."

Okay, her best friend was skeptical, which was not surprising for Analyse. Their conversation only made Kate feel more restless about wanting to go back into Time Out Woods. But before she did, Kate wanted a second opinion.

She found Ms. Lee in her homeroom. Ms. Lee pulled a chair next to her desk and invited Kate to sit. Kate took a deep purposeful breath, thinking about what she would say and how to say it.

"I want to talk to you about imagination," Kate began, rubbing her palms nervously on her lap. "Because I know it's your favorite topic, right?" Even though Kate believed this was about more than the imagination, she thought calling it that was the best way to break the ice and get Ms. Lee's attention.

Ms. Lee brightened, somewhat surprised. "You read me right. That's my passion."

"So, do you think there's another world? I mean, one we don't usually see, but like it's been there all the time?" Kate asked.

"Wow, you've been thinking." Ms. Lee leaned forward. "Absolutely I do. You know that poem, 'Who can see the wind, neither you nor I'? It means we can see the effects, and we call it wind, but we never actually see the wind even though it's there all the time."

"But do you think our imagination can play tricks on us? Make us, like, see things just because we want to see them?"

"Sure. But I don't think we could imagine anything if there weren't some truth about it, tricks or no tricks."

"But what we imagine is not real, right? So if it's just imagination, it's like a lie."

"A lie? No, I wouldn't call it that. The imagination or dreams are as real as what we call "facts" like trees and molecules. People might say, 'I just go by the facts, I only believe what I can see and touch.' That's baloney. Nobody lives that way. Throughout each day, we trust, we make guesses, we hope, we believe," she said with a smile, "and we *imagine.*"

"No," Kate said flatly. "It's not just my imagination. What if we could actually go *into* this other world? Like really *go* there?"

"You don't mean physically go there, do you?"

"Well . . . yeah, that is what I mean," Kate said.

"I see." Ms. Lee paused. "What got you thinking about all these great questions?"

Kate shifted in her seat. "I don't know. Just thinking about stuff."

"Kate, I know you've had a hard time at home. It's an adjustment. I know you love your dad . . . "

So her mom had talked with Ms. Lee, obviously. "Yes," Kate nodded.

"That may be what this is about. But let me just say this . . . it's okay to hope and believe and yes, imagine."

Kate went quiet for a moment, thinking. Sure, she missed her dad, but missing her dad couldn't explain the Kingdom of What Is. If it was all simply her imagination, she didn't want any part of it. She wanted what she could actually see and hear and touch. Like animals and people really understanding each other, even communicating, and clean ponds and palaces and lush grass fields with flowers of every color. And having her dad at home for real, not just imagining him at the other end of the phone!

That night Kate called Analyse.

"Meet me in the park on your way to school tomorrow," Kate said. "We have to talk."

"What about?"

"You'll find out when you get there. See you."

Chapter 4

Out of Time

Kate couldn't sleep. She turned on her light and took a spiral notebook from her backpack. She ripped out the pages of math problems and social studies questions to start a clean, fresh notebook. On the front cover she wrote in large letters, *The Kingdom of What Is Journal*. Opening to the first page, she wrote,

> *I'm totally freaking out. I don't understand what's going on in the woods, but I can't stop thinking about it. Even if Analyse is right about a spell, I'm going back.*
>
> *Animals talk there. It's not all in my head!*
>
> *I'm calling the beaver Budsley—he said something was amiss. Must find out what that gunk is.*
>
> *Took a ride on some geese. (Can't believe I just wrote that!) It was incredible (yes I mean "unbelievable" except how can I not believe it when I was actually riding on them!?) Geese are better than a plane because you can fly with the window open. (ha ha!)*
>
> *The castle turned out to be a dud. Just broken down ruins with a few tourists coming and going. A big disappointment, but maybe I should be done with princesses and ferries and castles at my age. Hey, I'm turning 13 this week!*
>
> *Some of those humans were spooky, like ghosts. Don't even know if they're real.*
>
> *First lesson—Don't drink the water.*
> *Second lesson—Time DOES stand still—in What Is.*
>
> *Next assignment:*
> *1. Find out what the stuff in the water is ??*

2. Find some humans to talk to.

3. Get Analyse to come with me. That will be a hard nut to crack because she thinks I'M the nut!

Kate had been writing so intently she did not notice her door open slightly. Two dark eyes peered in. Beneath those eyes appeared two other eyes near the floor. She quickly stuffed her notebook under her blankets.

"What do you want!" she snapped.

The door opened further. A little head with a cowlick poked inside. It was Gavin and Norbert their cat.

"Why is your light on?" Gavin asked.

"I can't sleep. Just leave already, will you?"

"What are you writing?"

"You don't need to know."

"I can't sleep. I'm thinking about Dad."

Kate sighed and told him to climb up into her bed, where he curled up next to her.

"You can sleep here, just don't fidget," she said turning off the light and crawling under the covers. She stared into the dark. "It's okay, I miss him too."

When she thought he was asleep, she tucked her notebook under her mattress. No, she wouldn't tell him anything because he would tell Mom, and after that the rest of the world would know, and then it would be all over for her. Some things little brothers should not be involved in.

The next morning before school, dependable Analyse met Kate at the poop tree as arranged. Before Analyse could ask any questions, Kate grabbed her by the hand and told her to run. In less than a minute they were across the park and stood at the wild rose bushes at the edge of the woods.

Analyse pulled up her nose. "If we're going in, why don't we use the normal trail over there. This is silly."

"Just follow me," Kate said, pushing her way through the briars. Her pack snagged on the way through.

Once on the other side, she turned to help Analyse, who was not there. Kate ducked back out and looked up and down the edge of the woods. She must have gone in at the trail entrance. She would meet her inside. Quickly back through the rose bushes, Kate found the trail where she hoped to intercept Analyse. If Analyse headed to Burton Pond as planned, she would have to come right down the trail where Kate was standing. She heard Analyse shouting for her in the distance.

"Over here, Lyse. Just keep following the path."

"Kate, quit playing games. Where are you?"

Finally, Kate caught a glimpse of her through the trees, coming down the trail toward her.

"Analyse! You found me. I thought—"

"Kate, where are you!" Analyse shouted again as she passed right through Kate as if she weren't even there. Kate gasped, feeling suddenly immersed in a cold vacuum. Analyse was unable to hear, see, or feel her! Analyse turned and ran back down the path, passing through Kate again, to the trail head where she had entered. Kate pushed her way back out through the wild roses. Analyse stood at the trailhead looking befuddled. Kate waved for her and she came running.

"I said follow me in! Why didn't you follow?"

"That way was easier," Analyse said.

Kate had to explain what she now understood as plainly as the nose on her face. "Lyse, listen to me, and you have to believe me. Through these bushes is the only way in. You went into Time Out Woods, the way everyone goes, but you didn't go into the Kingdom of What Is."

Analyse wrinkled her nose and shook her head.

Kate said, "When you were looking for me, I was right there and you . . . you didn't even see me. You like . . . passed right through me. Don't ask me why, but the only way to get in is right here." Now Kate understood why Time Out Woods seemed like the same old woods on her walk to Rocky Mound with her brother, her mom, and godfather Dennis. They'd all gone in at the marked trail head rather than through the rose hedge.

"I still don't have a clue what we're doing. Why are we here?" Analyse said.

"Check the time."

She checked her cell phone. "Okay, it's 8:45. Fifteen minutes before school starts. So what?"

"Just remember that."

Kate pulled aside the long briar stems for Analyse to go in, and she followed.

"Do you smell that?" Kate asked once they were in, taking a deep breath. The scent was even more pungent than what she'd smelled on her first visit. The smell reminded her of her dad's old leather briefcase. When she was a toddler, she used to stick her face into it and walk around with it over her head, papers spilling everywhere. It was one of those smells one never forgets.

Analyse breathed in a little, then pushed up her glasses. "Yeah?"

"So . . . ? Doesn't it smell different? Like powerful?"

"Uhm, it smells like woods. Just a guess."

They walked to the pond and paused. A couple of beavers were working on the far side.

"Okay," Analyse finally admitted. "It definitely feels a bit warmer and has kind of a summery smell."

"Right. And the leaves on the trees—they're still green, but this is the middle of October. Is that weird or what?"

"Oh, right."

"And look at the pond. Know what this is? It's Burton Pond, where people dumped all their old bikes and fridges and stuff."

"Wait, this is that dirty old pond?" Analyse said. "It can't be."

They peered into the pond and could see fish, some very large, swimming in and out among the plants below the surface. Swallows darted everywhere over the water. Burton Pond was never this clean.

"It's exactly the same place, Burton Pond, a little bigger maybe."

"Okay, you're starting to freak me out, Kate. We just hit a warm spot in the woods. And this may or may not be Burton Pond, but Kingdom of whatever . . . no. Let's go. We're late."

"Okay, we can go back. But first, we have to promise we won't tell anyone about this."

"Sure, whatever," Analyse said.

As they started back, they heard voices behind them near the pond. A man and woman were there with backpacks.

"How far is it?" the woman was asking.

"About six miles." The man stopped and unfolding a map. "We go along a farmer's field here for a ways and then on this trail to the ocean. Some people say there's some ruins there. But we won't get there today, we'll have to camp."

The woman looked over the pond. "I don't see why they don't do something about all this garbage. People just keep dumping their old tires and everything here . . . look, there's a lawnmower . . . gross."

The girls ran back to the pond and approached the two hikers.

"Hi," Kate said. "Where are you guys going?"

Neither of them heard her. They didn't even glance her way and walked on. A beaver stuck its head out of the water and stared at Kate and Analyse for a moment.

"Back again, eh?" It was Budsley. He coughed and looked a bit more worn and haggard than before. He glanced over his shoulder. "Those people? I'd expect them back by tomorrow when they're tired of it."

Analyse pulled up her nose at the beaver and stepped back. "What's that thing doing?"

"Beg your pardon," said Budsley. "Thing? That may be the common perception, but we do a lot around here which other *things* just take for granted."

It was obvious Analyse could not hear Budsley.

"Were those people going to the castle by any chance?" Kate asked Budsley.

"Are you talking to it, Kate?" Analyse was alarmed.

"Shh, keep listening," Kate said.

"They're typical Looky-Loo's," Budsley said. "They come and go, thither and yon, look around and leave. Few of them ever get to the center of things. If they do, they come back grumbling and tired and disappointed."

Suddenly, Analyse said, "I heard something."

"Good," Kate smiled. "Now just focus. It gets clearer as you listen, and you'll start to hear his voice."

Budsley continued, "Those Looky-Loo's can't hear you because you're probably not one of them. Perhaps you're the real thing—true blue travelers."

Analyse was nearly hyperventilating, realizing she was hearing Budsley's voice becoming clearer. She attempted to converse.

"Where are we?" she asked, deliberately and loudly, enunciating each word as though she were talking to an old person whose hearing was failing. "Where—is—this?"

Budsley scratched vigorously behind one ear with his back foot, gave Analyse an annoyed look, grabbed a twig, and dove under.

Analyse stood gaping, trying to take in that she was trying to converse with a beaver. She turned as if to run.

"Lyse, wait a second. Take a look at the time."

Analyse checked. "What? My clock must be broken." She tapped her phone. Kate held up her watch to compare. They both read 8:45. Analyse looked like she had just landed on an undiscovered planet—the Time Out

Woods she thought she knew was beginning to take the form of someplace else less familiar, the same but more marvelous.

Kate faced her with her hands on her hips and said firmly, "Okay, now tell me we're under some kind of spell. Tell me we're just imagining all this."

Analyse was visibly trembling. Her mouth was open but nothing came out. She sat down on the bank of the pond until she could finally gather herself enough to speak.

"I smell it now, Kate. The air, it's so pure and powerful it's frightening. It's so, I don't know . . . real," she said to Kate, to herself, and to the woods. "I don't know why but I feel like crying."

Kate nodded. "Like you've never felt more free, and like you might never feel tired again?"

Analyse said slowly, "So, time stops here. And when we go back out *there* . . . "

"School hasn't even started yet," Kate said, "and will never start as long as we're here. We're out of time in Time Out Woods . . . but we'll never be out of time because we have all the time in the world."

The girls laughed at the irony until they were rolling. As far as the world out there was concerned, it was as if they'd never left and they would not be missed.

Analyse jumped to her feet. "Where to now?" she asked, her face more bright and alert than Kate had seen it for a very long time. Kate smiled. She had gained a companion in her quest.

They looked left and right. Kate's eye caught a familiar looking trail on the other side of the dam to their right.

"There! Remember Miner's Gulch? That's the trail we took."

A creek flowed out from the pond over the dam. Across this creek was a trail that disappeared into the woods. Analyse did remember—the long walk with Kate and her dad up to the large pit. People had dug many years for gemstones and gold there and usually came back with nothing but an itch to go back and find what they were looking for. Analyse, Kate, her dad, and his university friend panned for gold in a stream at the bottom of the gulch. After two hours they had returned home with nothing but a couple of agates.

"Remember those carvings we found there?" Kate asked, thinking back to their hike. "My dad went back again with his friend, but they couldn't find them again because they were covered by a land slide."

"Do you think we'd find gold there now?" Analyse wondered.

"We'll never know standing here," Kate said, excited they were thinking along the same lines.

They started off on the trail to Miner's Gulch even though they were not sure if the gulch would even be there, let alone contain gold or precious stones. It was enough for Kate that she had a companion on her journey, her best friend. They had each other in a land they knew nothing of but had all the time in the world to discover.

Chapter 5

Miner's Gulch

Analyse bent down, scooped up some water from the stream, and let it run through her hands.

"Analyse, don't drink that! The black stuff I told you about?"

As they looked more closely, they could see it—a dark ribbon snaking downstream with the current, much thicker than what Kate had seen before. She grabbed a stick and pushed it into the mysterious, oozing gunk. In seconds the stick shriveled to a fragile blackened twig. Analyse jumped back.

"What is that?"

"It's destroying the pond. And I promised Budsley I'd tell the King and Queen."

"You never said anything about any king and queen."

"Because I didn't know if it was true, and I didn't want you to think I was making up some fairy tale. But now that you're here and you're convinced . . . "

Kate and Analyse took drinks from the water bottles in their packs and continued walking. The trail looked different from the way she remembered it, but it was taking them in the right direction.

They were feeling light on their feet. From the dam, they followed the stream east. A few minutes later, both girls recognized the trail that branched off sharply left uphill to Miner's Gulch. They ascended a winding path through hemlocks and firs. Two hours later, they heard water falling, which grew louder as they approached. The water came from a fissure in a rock and dropped into a large pool. Water striders skidded across the pool, and dragonflies zipped back and forth. The air was growing much warmer as they progressed upward, while it should have actually been getting cooler.

"I don't remember the climb being this steep," said Kate as she shed her hoodie and stuffed it in her pack. "And it's really getting hot."

"I don't remember these falls either. It's like a little paradise," said Analyse.

They stretched out by the pool and dug into the lunches they'd brought for school. They ate most of them and suddenly felt enormously tired. The initial energy they had had took them farther than they normally could have walked. They drifted quickly off into naps, however briefly, because moments later they were woken by the sound of small birds flitting up and down among branches by the falls.

"Kinglets!" Kate said. "Look, there's more of them further up the trail."

Analyse groaned. "Your kinglets ruined my nap."

The birds were chirping frantically around their heads until the chirping sounded to Kate like actual words. "Skip it, skip it." they kept repeating.

"Weird," Kate said. "They're probably warning us not to drink the water."

"I don't hear any actual words," Analyse said, moving closer to the kinglets. "Yes, I can now! They are saying 'skip it.'"

Kate called from further up the trail, "Lyse! Come quick!"

Analyse started up the trail just as a thick fog rolled over the crest of the mountain and enveloped them.

"Over here!" Kate yelled, her voice smothered by the cloud.

When the fog dissipated, there was Analyse only a few feet away. Kate was standing at the edge of a cliff.

"Look at this! I think it's Miner's Gulch," Kate said, "or kind of."

Analyse gasped when she looked over the edge. This was not a little gulch but a very deep, very wide canyon. They could make out some familiar contours and features of Miner's Gulch in the canyon walls the same way one might look at an old baby picture and recognize the face of the grown person that baby had become. But this was not exactly the Miner's Gulch they knew.

"I think I know where this is," Kate said. "The rock carvings we found with my dad were right down there. Let's check it out."

The trail they'd been hiking dropped into the canyon along steep walls. They followed it down, with careful steps, staying as far from the edge of the trail as they could. The farther they descended the warmer the air became.

They saw the kinglets again, flitting back and forth in front of them from rock to rock. "Skip it, skip it!" they chirped. Just then, the fog—or was it smoke—billowed up from below. This time the cloud was accompanied by an awful stench. And it was not cool as most fog is but so warm it caused them to sweat. They covered their noses and held on to the rock face to keep their balance.

Waiting in the fog, nearly blinded, Kate felt something she hoped had left her and would never return—the dark cloud that had smothered her after her dad left was creeping in again. She was paralyzed in her tracks and feared being stuck on the edge of the canyon with no way out but to jump into the cloud. She had a sudden urge to go home. But what was home without her dad?

A couple of minutes waiting and holding their noses felt like a couple of hours before the fog finally cleared and Kate stopped shaking. Analyse noticed beneath her hand there were grooves cut in the rock face—etchings of some kind.

"Kate, what is this?"

"That's it, the carvings I saw with my dad!"

"But what the heck does it mean?"

There were other carvings also, even more distinct than these. They looked like the petroglyphs in ancient tombs. One prominent figure was monster-like with smaller stick figures beneath it in lying positions and others kneeling as if praying. Lines radiated out from the central figure like shafts of sunlight. As their fingers passed over the carvings, the stone crumbled slightly as though they had been recently carved.

"Whoa, don't look down," Analyse said, looking over her shoulder.

The path they stood on dropped off sharply. The wind had dispersed the fog enough to give them a clear view of the canyon's full expanse. The upper end of the canyon was to their right and widened out in front of them to form a large bowl. And there on the floor of the canyon they saw the origin of the smoke—a large square structure with a door, like some kind of giant kiln or furnace. Around this furnace were stacks of building materials, and beyond those was an area that looked like it was under construction. In several places there lay piles of rock chiseled square, perhaps quarried from the sides of the canyon. The ground itself all around was exposed and scorched.

Most curious was a large pool that began at the furnace and stretched westward to their left, almost as long as a football field. This in itself would not be that strange were it not for the color of the water in the pool—milky white with bright yellow swirls.

"It's a little Grand Canyon, only really ugly," said Analyse.

"Look at that weird-colored water," Kate said. "You might say it's pretty, but it's not normal, so bizarre. The whole place, it's like a factory or something."

Along the length of the entire valley they could see no signs of life—no trees or animals or homes of any kind—until they noticed several people milling about by the large kiln. The smoke came billowing up once again and covered them, forcing them back up the trail.

"Keep moving," Kate said. "Just make sure your feet are on the path and stay close to the wall."

Hand over hand, slowly they found their way back up the path to the rim of the canyon. Once on safe ground, with the smog receding, they began running back down the trail. After a few minutes, they stopped out of breath. Where they stood, nothing looked familiar. Somehow they'd gotten off the main trail.

"Kate, where are we?"

Kate did not respond.

"That's it, I'm calling my mom." Analyse nervously fumbled in her pack for her cell phone.

"Are you nuts? What are you going to say? 'Hey Mom! We're lost in the Kingdom of What Is, can you pick us up?'"

Analyse dialed and glanced down at her phone. "It's not working. That's crazy, we're only a few miles from home."

"Lyse, think. There's no cell towers. We're not even in the same world as Shelby."

They could not tell how long they'd been gone, but it felt like at least four hours. They had come a long way, and they had no idea how or where they'd gone off the main trail.

Analyse started to cry. "This was a mistake, this place is dangerous. We can't drink the water, we can't even breathe . . . "

"And we can't give up yet," Kate said, trying to convince herself as well as Analyse. "Just remember the first feeling we had, right—how beautiful it was, the free feeling? Think about it. Would you rather be sitting in class with Dunphy talking about molecules?"

"Kate, did you remember we have a math test today?"

"Or never," Kate said. "Remember, today in Shelby is forever here. Math can wait."

Kate looked around to see if she could recognize anything in the area. "Stay here. I want to have a look."

Further ahead Kate disappeared through an opening in the trees. In a couple of minutes, she returned and quickly put on her pack. "Come on," she said, helping Analyse up.

"Where are we going?"

Kate led the way, half running and soon stood at the edge of the canyon again.

"No, Kate. Not this," Analyse pleaded.

They were further down the canyon away from the furnace, which meant less smoke. They stood on a broad rock shelf with a clear, majestic view. Directly below them, a river snaked from the construction area westward through a narrowing in the canyon. It eventually ran into a broad open valley farther to their left. They could see the yellowish water from the construction pond being carried in the stream's flow. The yellow turned a darker brown as it mixed with the silt in the river.

Not far from where they stood, in the canyon wall, was the opening to a cave.

Kate pointed. "I think I've been in there."

The girls entered the cave cautiously, letting their eyes adjust to the darkness. They could make out an area wide enough for several people to take shelter. There were charred pieces of wood in a fire pit.

"This looks like someone's camp," Analyse said. "We can't stay here."

"We need to spend the night somewhere, and if someone comes back, maybe they can tell us what's going on down in the canyon. We need to make friends here if we want to learn anything. And maybe they'll have something to eat."

As she said this, the light from the cave entrance suddenly dimmed and went bright again as if something or someone had passed by. Analyse quickly shrunk back into the cave.

"It was nothing," Kate said.

"You don't know that," Analyse said wide-eyed.

"Maybe not, but I know I don't want to try walking anymore in the dark, when we're not even sure where we are."

The sun was angling low and the air was cooling. Kate poked at the charred wood in the fire pit.

"Let's look for wood and see if we can light a fire." Just as Kate said this, she realized she had brought no matches. "Forget it." She sighed and sat down with her arms wrapped around her knees and rested her head.

Moments later a light went on inside the cave, and Kate jumped to her feet. It was Analyse, holding up a lighter. Kate stared in disbelief.

"I still have this in my pack," Analyse said, "from the me-and-Jeremy days."

Analyse proved to be a good fire builder. Using paper from her school notebook and dry bits of wood along with the partially burned logs, she quickly had a small fire going. The girls pulled their hoodies tightly over their heads and huddled closely together. Their stomachs rumbled. They combined what was left in their lunches—two granola bars, a few grapes, some dried seaweed, and the rest of the water in their water bottles. It was enough for the night. The glow of the fire danced across their faces.

"Did you really camp with Jeremy?" Kate asked.

"A few times."

"Where?"

"Behind the warehouse, in that tree lot. It was our secret spot."

"Gross."

"We escaped our houses after dark and would build a fire out there and just sit and talk . . . the whole night. He's loquacious."

"Lo-quack-what?"

"He talks a lot. When it started getting light, we would run home before our parents woke up. I hated smoking though. I smoked just to be with him. Now he's in grade ten, and I'm still a lowly grade eight. It's like I don't exist."

"Forget about him. Isn't that what you told me I should do about Nolan?"

"Kate, you're not even thirteen yet."

"I will be. You're *barely* thirteen."

"So you never thought about Nolan before, like I did about Jeremy?"

"I guess so, but not since I came into Time Out Woods and found . . . all this. It feels good not to think about boys. The world has got much bigger."

The girls were quiet for a long time, staring into the fire.

"Kate, remember the kinglets? They were trying to stop us from going down into that canyon, I bet. And we didn't listen."

"Don't worry about it, we're good now."

Their conversation trailed off into exhausted silence, and they slept with their heads leaning against each other. They woke chilled sometime in the middle of the night when the fire died down. As Analyse put on some fresh wood, they heard tumbling rocks, followed by hurried footsteps that trailed off in the distance. Their sleep was fitful the rest of the night.

The mouth of the cave shone like a spotlight when the sun rose in the morning. Kate reached for her pack.

"Lyse, our packs. They're gone."

They scanned the cave. There was no sign of them until they came out of the cave onto the ledge and discovered both packs sitting open. Their contents were scattered—their caps, water bottles, school books—but nothing had been taken.

"Look at this," Analyse said, "somebody was curious."

Lying open on a rock was Kate's science book, held open by two stones. Someone had been examining these pages. There were dirty fingerprints over the diagrams of the solar system.

"What would anyone want with a boring old science book?" Analyse said.

"And why the pictures of outer space?"

"Let's get out of here, this is creeping me out," Analyse said as she stuffed her things back into her pack.

"But whoever it was didn't hurt us, think about it," Kate said. "What are we afraid of?"

"That for instance."

Analyse pointed down into the canyon. Three carts were being drawn by horses up the valley toward the furnace. They were guided by men in red uniforms, and sitting in the carts were people. The carts moved past the yellow-white pond and stopped near the construction site. From this distance, the figures below looked like toys as the girls watched the people pile out of the carts and go to various jobs. The ones in red suits directed them—some to the furnace, others to the material piles, and others to the actual construction area. There were at least thirty workers. The base of the structure was a large square, made of large stones, covering almost an entire city block.

"What would anybody be building way up here in the middle of nowhere?" Kate asked.

"Well, I don't want to find out," Analyse said.

"I'm starving," Kate said. "We need to find something to eat."

Analyse said. "Well, I didn't see any 7-Elevens on the way up. We have to go back."

They retraced their steps in search for the place where they had lost the original trail when they noticed someone peering at them from the bushes. They ran.

"Who was that?" Analyse said when they finally stopped to catch their breath.

Kate tried to assume the best. "Maybe they didn't mean any harm."

A few minutes later, they found the spot where they had veered off course toward the cave, and three hours later they had made their way back to Budsley's pond, tired and hungry.

In spite of their horrid discovery of the canyon, Kate felt a sense of confidence. They had survived the smoky cliff, stayed overnight in a cave, and had witnessed a strange building project. Kate only hoped that Analyse felt the same and would not desert her.

Near the wild rose hedge Kate stopped at the strawberry patch she'd found on her first visit. She bit into a deep red berry. The juice spread like a crimson sunrise in her mouth. She wanted to remember this taste, savoring it before following Analyse out through the bushes to Shelby.

Chapter 6

White Noise

From Wild Rose Passage to school was less than ten minutes at a slow walk. No one else had arrived. Their heads were aching from lack of food. They scoured the shelves above the lockers and found four discarded lunch bags with a few left over items that looked reasonably edible.

Mr. Dunphy's science class was their first of the day. No one would be there for another five minutes. They stuffed themselves with chunks of sandwich, carrot sticks, and brownies, glancing furtively down the hall between bites like two wolf children. After filling themselves, they fell instantly asleep at their desks and didn't wake up until they felt someone's fingers tapping on their heads.

It was Nolan. "Hey, what are you guys doing? Did you stay overnight here?"

Students were filing in. Before Mr. Dunphy arrived, the girls had their heads back down on their desks, asleep again. A few minutes later they bolted awake, almost falling out of their seats at the sound of an explosion. This was followed by the dry, resonant voice of Mr. Dunphy.

"Now, everyone," he said, "what was the difference between the sound of my pencil dropping to the floor and that sound of the balloon popping? Which by the way, I notice, just brought our two friends back to the land of the living."

The class stared at Kate and Analyse and laughed.

"Analyse, what do you think? Could you hear my pencil dropping?"

"Uh, no," she said.

"No, you couldn't. Why not?"

Analyse gazed bleary-eyed. Obvious to everyone, she couldn't hear it because she was asleep. "Uhm," she said, "because the pencil forgot to scream as it was falling?"

Everyone but Dunphy laughed. Analyse could be cheeky even in a half-sleep.

"Yes, well," said Dunphy, not amused, and raised his eyebrows. "One reason is, our brains get used to the sound waves in a certain environment, the sound waves in this room for instance. And our brains adjust to these familiar sounds—paper shuffling, chalk on the board, people's movements, pencils dropping, and we just shut these sounds out. We effectively don't hear them."

They were used to Dunphy rambling on about things he thought should interest them. The balloon popping—that was exciting, but now he was losing their attention.

"You even shut out the sound of my voice sometimes, and your brains just . . . fall asleep," he joked and grinned crookedly, looking a little hurt. No one laughed.

"We assume," Dunphy droned on, "these familiar sounds are not worth our notice because they're so ordinary. But when an unfamiliar sound is introduced, like a balloon going bang for instance, you notice it even in a deep sleep. Thus, the difference between what we call "white noise," which some people use to help them sleep, and alarm clocks, which of course people use to wake themselves up. But as we know, even alarm clocks can become ordinary and may fail to do the trick."

Kate, for once, found herself drawn in by what Dunphy was saying. Yes, white noise was what she was hearing right here—at school and home—people talking about stuff that wasn't important. Maybe the real sound people should be paying attention to was not here but in the Kingdom of What Is, and people just couldn't hear it. She raised her hand.

"About sound . . . " she started, gathering her thoughts, "what happens when sound travels from one time to another time? Is there still sound?"

Dunphy raised his eyebrows, attempting to understand whether Kate was really asking a question or trying to be funny. Fearing he might be taking the bait and falling into a trap, he ventured a question in return. "You mean from earth's atmosphere to outer space, for example? The way some people think they hear aliens?"

Everyone was paying attention again.

"No," Kate said, "I mean from our time to the time of another world. Could we hear sound . . . or voices coming from another world different from the world we're sitting in now?"

Analyse whispered, "Kate, are you nuts? You're going to spill everything."

Kate persisted with Dunphy. "What if you and me—just imagining I mean—what if we were in different worlds right now? Then we might not be able to hear each other, right? We might be talking, but we just wouldn't hear each other. Like 'white noise,' right?"

There were more odd stares and a few snickers.

"You and I in different worlds, completely talking past each other, yes," Dunphy said sarcastically. "Kate, whatever you're thinking, we live in the same universe, whether either of us like it or not, and we live by the same rules of physics."

She was not trying to be funny. Her mind was racing in the Kingdom of What Is. Why did the "Looky-Loos" not hear the girls, and why could they not hear Budsley at first? And why did Analyse not hear her at first? She was curious what someone like Dunphy would say, and now she knew—there were some things that even the smart guys couldn't explain.

"Could I ask about something else?" she said. "You were talking about 'pie' yesterday in math. If pie is an infinite number, then circles must be infinite too, right, and go on forever." She shaped her hands in a circle to illustrate, slowly extending them outward.

Nolan looked over at Kate dumbfounded. This was not the quiet, reserved Kate he had known. Dunphy took a moment to clear his throat and rub his chin. Just to end the conversation, he admitted that she might have a point, then looked at the clock and dismissed the class.

During library period, Kate and Analyse sat by themselves looking over Kate's Kingdom of What Is Journal. On two facing pages, with Analyse's help Kate sketched a map with the important landmarks they had discovered so far. She drew in the rose hedge and wrote "Wild Rose Passage." She drew in the pond and labeled it "Budsley Pond," and "Singing Meadow" as well for where she'd met the throng of geese. She added "Miner's Gulch," drawing in a large cloud of smoke with a question mark in the middle of the cloud. Analyse said to add "Stranger's Cave," which they named after the strange person that had visited them at night.

Kate did not mark the location of the palace. Not only was she unsure if it was really the palace but also, having flown there, she didn't exactly

THE KINGDOM OF WHAT IS

know *where* it was. She drew a large question mark in the empty space to the north and west, which still had to be explored.

"If you're thinking of going anywhere near that canyon again," Analyse stated firmly, "I'm not going."

"We don't have to go to the canyon. Let's go over here next," Kate said, putting her pencil down on her question mark north of Singing Meadow. "If we've got this right, the ocean should be over here," she said pointing a little further west on the map. The more they worked on the map, the more excited they became about going back. But this time they would go equipped with extra food.

When Kate arrived home after school, she overheard her mom in the kitchen on the phone. She knew immediately it was her dad, and her heart sank expecting another fight.

"But this is what we agreed," she was saying. "You told me what if you just left and I agreed you should—you know you couldn't get custody, you haven't even—of course they miss you, but all this was your—" There was another pause before her mom hung up without saying anything else.

Kate walked into the kitchen, where her mom was hanging her head, her phone beside her on the counter.

"Was that dad on the phone?"

"Yes," her mom said, wiping her face, and tried to turn the conversation. "But the call I need to talk to you about is the one from Mr. Brodeur."

Apparently, according to Brody as the students called their school principal, Mr. Dunphy thought Kate's sleeping in class was responsible for her lower scores as well as some of her odd behavior. He deemed it serious enough to tell Principal Brody, who then thought it was worth calling her mom about.

Kate's little brother, Gavin, appeared at the bottom of the stairs with an impish smile and said, "You're toast."

They were all "concerned," her mom explained, about her daydreaming and doodling and sleeping in class. The worst thing was that she had been getting D's and F's. "This is just not like my daughter," her mom reminded her, "far below your potential. You're not necessarily an A student, but failing?"

Her mom went on about things at home: Kate's bedroom looked like it had been hit by a hurricane, which was also "just not her," and her usual chores weren't getting done. Her mom held up a grammar worksheet she'd found in Kate's backpack.

"What are these drawings on your worksheet? It has nothing to do with grammar. "

"What were you doing in my backpack?" Kate snatched the paper from her mom's hand. "They're just doodles, everyone doodles."

"It's what's *not* on the papers—the correct answers. Kate, you know this stuff."

Her mom showed her another sheet with more doodles. "A castle? And what's this here?" She put her finger on what looked like pictures of explosions. "That's a bit scary. Why are you drawing bombs? That's unspeakable." There was alarm in her voice. "Honey, is this some kind of acting out? Is it because of your dad?"

Kate didn't have a sensible response for any of her questions.

She also wanted to know about the library books Kate brought home—books about time flight, adventure books, and books about living in the woods. These subjects were very out of the ordinary for her.

"Well, whatever it is, you need to get back on track with your school work. You can't just let this go."

That night Kate tried calling her dad. This time he had his phone on. His voice sounded worn. He said he'd been marking lots of essays, but Kate knew that wasn't why he was tired.

He asked, "Why are you in bed already?"

"Just tired I guess, like you," she said. "Why can't you and Mom just stop fighting and come home?"

"We're sorting some things out, but I'll be back soon." It was the same old line.

"It doesn't sound like you'll be back soon. I overheard your phone call with Mom."

There was a pause. "Your mom said something about your schoolwork. What's going on?"

Kate told him about the call from Principal Brodeur and everything her mom had said.

"Well, the word 'normal' has never suited you, but that doesn't bother me," her dad said. "You've always been interested in more than just what was in the textbooks. It's what any teacher wishes from a student." Her dad wondered if her poor performance was because she was interested in a particular boy, and he reminded her she'd soon be thirteen years old and to be interested in boys was quite okay.

"No, Dad. It's not about boys." She took a deep breath. She felt she needed to come clean on a few things. "Can you promise not to tell anyone about something, not even Mom?" she said.

"Of course. It's confidential."

"Uhm, I've been spending a lot of time in the woods. I went there today before school, and that's why I slept in class."

"That's it? There are far worse things than going into the woods. That's what this is about?" He laughed. "Curiosity is a good thing. What were you doing there?"

"Just exploring."

"Exploring?"

"It's just that I found another world there, Dad, and . . . and it's got into my head."

"That's good. You know that I've always wanted you to love the natural world—"

"No, it's not . . . I mean . . . yes, I love the woods, but this is different."

"You mean, you love it for its spiritual qualities then?"

"Something like that I guess, but Dad, you know when you said there's a lot more to Time Out Woods than most people see?"

"Yes."

"It's true." She went on to tell about how the woods she discovered was much larger than the Time Out Woods they knew, and how time stopped when she was there, even if she would stay for half a day!

Her dad agreed, "It's a wonderful feeling when time seems to stop. I wish I felt that more often, to be honest."

She told him how beautiful it was, and how it smelled like his brief-case. She said how she'd found the carvings they'd once seen in Miner's Gulch. As she continued her story, she lost her fear of being found out. "The Gulch, wow, Dad, it's really just a small part of a huge canyon! And, you know that dirty old pond? It's just alive! The animals, they're talking to me."

"Okay," her dad said cautiously, trying to take in everything she was telling him. "You're not doing all this alone, are you?"

"No, with Analyse. It's safe, dad. We're not gonna get attacked or anything."

"That's good," he said. He reminded her that if she met with anyone suspicious to use her best assets—her brain and her legs. "Look, I'm glad you're exploring, but don't let it get in the way of your school work, alright? That's your first responsibility. I don't like to hear about failing marks.

Books give you the foundation, and curiosity gives you the growing edge. So yes, pursue both your books and the woods, but don't forget the first."

"Don't worry, Dad, it's not taking me away from class. Literally."

"While we're talking about sneaking out of school," he said, "let's go to Max's for a burger during your lunch hour Friday. It's your birthday."

"We only get forty minutes for lunch, Dad. Why can't you come home for my party Friday night?" Kate pleaded. "It's just me and Analyse and Mom and Gavin."

Her dad sighed. "Nice idea, but I don't think your mother would be ready for that. Let's do lunch Saturday instead. I'll talk to her."

There was the cloud again with its familiar sadness. Her dad couldn't even come to her thirteenth birthday party! Had to talk to her mom first? It was so stupid. She began fidgeting with her journal.

"Okay, bye," she said softly and hung up. She opened to a blank page in her journal and drew two large eyes, then scrawled a large dark mass over the entire page until the eyes had all but disappeared.

The shouts of soccer and basketball players from the park were subsiding. She looked out across the park to the woods. The sun was setting, casting a yellow October aura over the trees.

She wrote in her journal to get her mind off her mom and dad and home and Shelby.

What Is has got me. It's mysterious and amazing. But it's a mixed bag—light and darkness, beauty and danger, excitement and fear. But I don't care. It's more alive than here.

She may be totally weird, and she may even be running away, but she wanted desperately to go back there—dark smelly clouds and all.

Chapter 7

Corvus

Kate's mom had made an arrangement with Principal Brodeur. To get her grades back up, Kate would sit in Brody's lunch break detention, along with several other students in the same boat. They had fifteen minutes to eat their lunches and then had to sit with Brody for the remaining twenty-five minutes of the break. After two weeks, if Kate's grades came back up, she could discontinue detention.

Rather than try explaining how she didn't need the detention, Kate decided to keep the peace and color between the lines as she was told and do whatever it took to keep her visits to the woods a secret.

So the next day, Thursday, during detention Kate sat in silence with a handful of other students. Brody sat at the front of the room chewing furiously on a sandwich, sniffing loudly between bites, and entering data on his PC. Some students sat with their heads on their desks and their books propped up in front of them as shields against Brody's eyes. Others doodled or stared out the window. One or two actually studied. One thing made it somewhat bearable for Kate—her friend Nolan was there too.

"Who made you come here?" Kate asked him.

"Never mind. Happy birthday," he whispered and gave her a large chocolate he'd picked up from the specialty store.

"Thanks," Kate said. "But my birthday's tomorrow."

"I know. I got you something more than chocolate, but I'm giving it to you Saturday."

"Why can't you give it to me tomorrow on my birthday?"

"Not at school." He changed the subject. "What were you and Analyse talking about—going to 'time out' or whatever? What's that?"

"Are you spying on us?"

"Just curious, I heard you in the hall."

"That was about Gavin," Kate lied. "My mom's going to give him a time out if he pokes his nose into my business anymore."

Nolan didn't say anything else that sounded nosy, and Kate told him nothing, remembering her vow to secrecy.

Fifteen minutes into detention, Analyse's face appeared at the door. She handed Brody a slip of paper. The vice principal had sent her. Kate sat up in surprise. Analyse took a seat beside her.

"Shh!" Analyse said. "They caught me smoking."

"Dummy!" said Kate.

"I did it on purpose, I just wanted to keep you company."

Analyse slipped her a note. Kate smiled as she read it. Her best friend had not abandoned her. The note was a list including things Analyse thought they should take along on their next trip, with one word written large at the bottom with a question mark—"When?"

Kate crumpled the paper, her heart pounding, and dropped the note into her bag.

After school the girls planned their next getaway to the woods.

Kate said, "I really want to find out if there's really—"

"—I know, really a palace." Analyse finished her sentence, laughing. "You keep saying it."

Kate said, "Wouldn't it be awesome!" Kate was not sure if there was another, less dilapidated, palace than the one the geese took her to, a more respectable palace perhaps. Or maybe she'd just been too high up in the sky to give it a fair look and needed to see it up close.

"Yeah, of course. It would be amazing!" Analyse said. "Meeting a real king and queen in a big old palace with jewels and velvet robes."

"Plus, I promised Budsley."

"We should go tomorrow," Analyse said, "as your birthday present!"

It was agreed. The next day, Friday, Kate and Analyse had just sat down in the lunch room for the fifteen minutes before their detention with Brody. Without opening their lunches, the girls got up from their table and slipped on their backpacks. Nolan saw them pass by and stopped chewing, wondering why they were cutting out of lunch so soon. Detention wouldn't be starting yet.

Once out of the lunch room, the girls half ran down the hall and slipped out a side door that led onto the school grounds. The door had no sooner closed behind them when it opened again. It was Gary, the school janitor.

"In a hurry? You know you're not supposed to be out here till the bell rings, right?"

"Uhm," Analyse said, "we're just . . . we just need a couple things, something really important . . . for our science project. Mr. Dunphy said it was imperative."

"Sure, right . . . science project . . . imperative. I didn't see anything." Gary mumbled something else and disappeared back inside.

They sprinted like a couple of escapees for the mesh fence that surrounded the school grounds, half expecting to be shot in the back. They squeezed through a gap in the fence and glanced over their shoulders. No one was following. As they were running past Shelby Elementary, they heard movement in the bushes and sped up. One block later, they were at Wild Rose Passage and quickly disappeared quicker than two foxes through the briars.

They had walked as far as Budsley Pond when they were suddenly interrupted by the call of a crow only a few feet above them.

"Look," Kate said, pointing up at a crow with one white wing feather.

"Yeah, a crow, so what?"

"Not just any crow," Kate said.

"Master Corvus, if you please," said the crow, as it dropped to a branch eye level with the girls. "Or simply Corvus."

Analyse jumped. She was speechless for a moment, ashamed for being so surprised after all she'd already seen.

"Off on an adventure, are we?" Corvus looked them over as if assessing whether or not they were prepared. "And who do we have the pleasure of her company today?"

Kate introduced Analyse, who managed a faint hello.

"Where has everyone gone?" Kate asked, looking over the pond, which appeared deserted by bird and beaver alike.

"Gone? Because you don't see them does not mean they've gone. They've learned, as we all have, there is a time to flee and a time to stay and fight, a time to take cover and a time to be known. Today is a time to take heed and hide."

Before another question could be asked, Corvus motioned with an extended wing to follow him to a large tree near the pond. At the base of the tree was a crevice covered over by a thatch work of twigs, which Corvus kicked away. In the crevice was a cache of dried roots.

Corvus said, "I can see you are on a mission. You should take some of these." He dropped a few roots at their feet, but the girls hesitated. "We crows don't eat them, but we stash them for travelers such as yourselves. The Ancients say they're better cooked, but they eat them raw, too. Just make sure to chew them up."

"Who are the Ancients?" Kate asked.

"People much like yourselves . . . people who are still loyal to the King and Queen. We know they pass through here occasionally because the roots are gone." Corvus scratched at the debris to cover up the cache again as his voice went very quiet. "I gather you are not fully aware of the rebellion against Athar."

"Against who?"

"Athar and Sapienta, the King and Queen."

"What rebellion?"

"The rebellion of Grod Vurmis—he started this Plague, and now it's making its way into every nook and cranny in the Kingdom. Some are taken by force and others simply give in to him, but they all become Vumis's slaves. Their names disappear from the land and their stories go with them. Only the Ancients have stayed."

"Where are they—the Ancients?"

"Not in these parts, but you would do well to find them as soon as you can and make them your friends."

Kate held her stomach, hearing of Grod Vurmis. "I got sick," Kate said, "from the water. Is that—?"

"The Plague," confirmed Corvus, "the work of Grod Vurmis. It's why you don't see a lot of activity around here at the moment. The beavers are masters at survival. They'll stay on top of things as well as any, but I fear there are not enough of them to hold back the Plague for much longer. And there are other areas of the Kingdom that have regretfully fared much worse."

"And the smoke?"

"Also the Plague, yes."

"We were at Miner's Gulch. It was awful," said Analyse.

"Miner who?"

"The canyon," Kate said, pointing. "It had some kind of furnace."

"The Great Gorge. My, you certainly do not shy from danger—a good sign for serious travelers. You are obviously in the lineage and tradition of the Ancients. The furnace is where he dines, so to speak, and gorges himself. Thus, it has become known as the Great Gorge."

"Gorging himself with what?" Analyse asked.

"Anything and everything, living or dead, anything he can put to his cause—for whatever he's making, for spreading his plague—even gorging on things he can't use, things he takes just because he can, out of spite."

Kate and Analyse screwed up their faces in disgust at the idea of someone so completely self-serving.

Corvus continued earnestly, "But far worse than any sickness you can imagine from water or smoke is the sickness from coming under the influence of Vurmis. If you were at the Great Gorge, I am surprised you didn't meet up with him. His minions patrol the entire area. They would have certainly tried to capture you, or preferably tried to deceive you into coming willingly."

Kate thought of the stranger by the cave.

"We're quite certain," Corvus said, "the Great Gorge is where Grod Vurmis is attempting to establish his center and advance his rebellion. You must resist him at every threat. Once he or his minions get hold of you, they will change you so you eventually won't even recognize yourself anymore. You'll have forgotten who you are and your whole purpose for being. And that is far worse than any physical illness you can imagine."

Kate's mind was racing. She thought of the smoke, the gunk, and the stillness of the pond.

"Have some of these roots," Corvus offered again. "Besides being very nutritious, they'll help you resist the Plague, not cure it mind you, just make your stomachs stronger against it. We're still searching for better remedies. But of course the only real remedy is destroying Grod Vurmis. Which is beyond my doing and far beyond what any roots or herbs can do."

The girls looked doubtfully at the dirty tubers lying at their feet and finally took several each and added them to their packs. They would have to listen and adapt to the ways of the land, thought Kate. They were not about to argue, especially if adapting might mean their survival.

"Stay close to the right path and listen to the right guides," Corvus told them. "If your purpose is noble and right, your journey cannot fail."

"The right guide like you?" Kate asked.

Corvus swayed with as much modesty as he could muster and cleared his throat with a low, drawn-out croak. "Of course, I would agree with that judgement. But, you never know if a guide is truly wise until your experience bears out what he says." Then he took flight beneath the tree boughs, and they were alone.

Kate had to admit that their "mission" was not as clear to them as Corvus may have assumed. Doubt was creeping in. She looked at Analyse, who seemed to be waiting for Kate to make a move. They had come for an adventure but had not counted on walking into a rebellion or a plague, or dealing with any Grod Vurmis.

"If you're too scared, we can go back," said Kate, who was scared herself at the thought of being without her best friend and companion in a quest they had so looked forward to undertaking.

Analyse was at a rare loss for words. Finally she sighed, "It's your call."

Kate went back in her mind over what she knew to this point. In spite of the danger, she was determined to discover more of this land and also help if they could. And even more so now, she wanted to find the palace and meet the King and Queen. Yes, it seemed more dangerous than they'd expected, but at least they could put names to what they had to face.

Without another thought, Kate simply began walking and Analyse followed. They moved quickly along the pond toward Singing Meadow. As they did, Kate felt pulled forward by something bigger than her own power. It was the same feeling she'd had when she first followed Corvus through the rose hedge into the woods.

On pure intuition, they climbed a grassy slope at the west end of Singing Meadow. This was roughly the direction the geese had taken Kate on her wondrous flight. They stopped at a scattering of boulders at the top of the hill. The trail took a fork here. One path continued west and the other veered right to the north over rolling hills. This was much different terrain than what they had to negotiate through woods up the mountain to the Great Gorge.

"Wait a minute," Kate said. "This is Rocky Mound, look."

The rocks where they were resting were the same rocks Kate had sat on many times. The surroundings, however, were grassy rather than the tall thistles and weeds she knew. Their view showed them a land that went far beyond Time Out Woods. This new land was vast. It seemed to be all-encompassing, including everything they knew and everything they did *not* know.

Kate took her journal from her pack to check the map she'd been working on. She traced her finger to her question mark in the blank space and looked north over the grass covered hills, which seemed to go on forever before they met with mountains in the distance.

They were glad for the lunches they'd taken with them and ate hungrily. They jumped suddenly when Corvus appeared and landed beside them.

"Not to interfere. Only wanted to make quite sure you were on the right track," Corvus said, eyeing their sandwiches. "On the topic of lunch, it was not my inclination to interrupt, only to perhaps join in."

Kate and Analyse did not pick up the hint.

"What I mean to say is, I would never refuse a sampling of delicacies transported here from foreign lands."

"Uh, oh . . . of course," said Kate, breaking off a piece of her ham and cheese sandwich and handing it to Corvus. He quickly picked it up in his beak and threw his head back, and it was gone in a couple of gulps.

"Excuse the manners," he said. "I rarely get a chance at fresh sandwich. The yellow stuff is interesting. Cheese, is it?" He smacked his beak a couple of times and shook his head as if something were stuck.

Analyse politely reached out with a piece from her own sandwich.

"Mm, tuna. Now that," said Corvus, smacking his beak several times, "*that* is worth a trip to your garbage can some day. Where do you live?"

The girls could not suppress their laughter. In the distance, they heard the sound of crows making a loud commotion.

"Never mind them," Corvus said. "They're in a heated debate over a large chunk of salmon carried up from the beach—arguing about who did the finding and who did the carrying and who deserves it. In the end the answer is always the same. Whoever did the finding or the bringing, everyone takes part in the reward."

"We need some help from a trusted guide," Kate said finally.

Corvus hopped to a higher rock and focused.

"Where is the palace from here?" she asked.

Corvus extended one wing with a glint of white, pointing north over the endless, rolling hills. "Definitely this way. The other trail there," he said pointing west, "leads you deeper into the woods until you reach the sea. That would get you there by a longer and more dangerous route over water. But I see you haven't brought your boat. So you definitely want the trail north. The palace is only three or four hours as the crow flies. As the girl walks, I'd say more than a couple of days. It's a meandering path, with plenty between here and there."

"Plenty of what?"

Corvus reflected. "Plenty of everything under the sun." He cocked his head sideways with one eye to the sky and the other to the earth. "You have reached the beginning of the middle."

"Middle of what?" asked Kate.

"Why . . . the middle of everything that is, I'd say."

"So where *is* the middle?" Analyse asked, looking for a straight answer.

Corvus preened his one white feather as if summoning wisdom from a talisman before he spoke. "It is where you want to be."

"Where we want to be?" Analyse asked, becoming frustrated. "Where is that?"

"I presume, if you're descendents of the Ancients, you want to be with the King and Queen, and they're always in the middle of things, believe me."

While Analyse took a few steps down the path for a better view, Kate considered the thought of a two-day journey on foot. She looked to the sky, remembering the geese.

Corvus leaned toward Kate. "The geese told me you got spooked when you saw the palace. Not to worry, outward appearances can be deceiving. I suggest you not give up and give it another try."

"Another goose ride?"

"Well, no, not recommended. Another goose transport for the ex-pressed purpose of an express passage would be the easiest way. But it would not be nearly as satisfying as making your own way there. A goose ride would only be like reading the last page of a book without reading all the parts in the middle. You'd miss all the fun of getting there and never be the wiser for it."

"Yes, maybe, but—" Kate began.

"Remember, pay attention to wise guides."

They were again interrupted by the chatter of crows in the distance.

"The clamorous horde calls," said Corvus, glancing in the direction of his friends. "If you'll excuse me, there's a quarrel I want to be a part of." He spread his wings and bowed chivalrously. "I thank you for your delectable bites." He rose and caught a breeze that swept him up and over Singing Meadow.

Chapter 8

Shadows

Kate and Analyse looked out across the hills and vast grasslands. There were copses of trees and shrubs here and there like patches on a pair of old jeans. A trek of more than two days would only be possible with the help of some miraculous energy and friends along the way. The trail Corvus had pointed them onto seemed to disappear at the crest of one hill into the wide, forever sky.

"That Corvus is an odd bird," remarked Analyse.

Kate said, "That's why I like him."

They smiled in agreement. They were buoyant from their meeting with Corvus and started off with a jump in their step on their path north.

Ten minutes later they looked back. Behind them was Singing Meadow and Budsley Pond, and Shelby was nowhere in sight. Kate shivered. She felt somehow she was leaving herself behind and would never be the same again. Glimmering in the afternoon light, something else made them shiver. There were several rivulets, like the one Kate had got sick from, which ran down the hills into Singing Meadow. From this angle, the small streams stood out as fine yellow streaks.

The rivulets became dark yellow as they flowed down toward the meadow, faded to brown streaks, and finally turned black in the meadow itself. It was as if they were watching the evolution of the gunk that all started at the Great Gorge. And it was worsening.

Kate put her hand to her water bottle. Where would they find more water when their bottles were empty? After an hour's walk, they began to see signs of human life dotting the landscape. Cultivated fields and farms and the occasional home appeared. They stood at the top of a prominent hill with a good view to all sides.

"It's awesome!" Analyse exclaimed. "Who knew all this existed on the other side of Time Out Woods?"

They heard shouting behind them and looked back to see a small boy climbing up the trail after them at a quick pace.

"Gavin!" Kate screamed in disbelief.

Gavin came puffing and panting up the path, his cowlick wagging. The girls stood and gaped.

"What are you doing here!" Kate shouted.

Gavin fell to the ground and sat, trying to catch his breath.

"How did you get here?" Analyse asked.

"I'm hungry," he said.

"My journal!" Kate cried. "You read my journal, didn't you!"

Gavin was silent.

"How did you find us?"

"I heard you on the phone to Analyse, you said you were taking off at lunch time. And it was all in your journal—the rose bushes, the talking crow, and the beaver!" Gavin said as if he'd uncovered a monumental conspiracy. "And you didn't tell me."

"Because it was none of your business!"

"I waited outside school in the bushes where I knew you'd be walking by, and I followed you." Gavin said. He'd caught criminals in the act, but now he was determined to join them.

Kate was red-faced with anger. "You violated my privacy!"

Analyse stood staring at him with her arms crossed.

"You can't come," Kate said, "so just get that out of your head. You don't know anything and you aren't prepared. You didn't even bring anything."

"I know about the Great Gorge."

Analyse leaned over to him at eye level and spoke in a low menacing voice. "You don't know anything about the Great Gorge. It's an awful place of smoke and darkness where nothing lives. And if you don't go home, we'll bring you there and leave you."

"I don't care, go ahead."

"It's no use," Analyse said, giving up. "He'll follow us to the gates of hell."

Gavin spoke ominously. "If you make me go back, I'm telling Mom."

Kate slugged him in the shoulder.

Gavin sobbed and held his shoulder. "Why do you always have to keep secrets? You think you're Dad's favorite, well you're not! You're not the only one that matters. You always think you can do stuff and leave me out, but I can do anything you can do!"

There was a long pause as the girls rolled their eyes and wondered what to do.

Finally Analyse said, "He'll tell everything. We have to take him."

"You can come," said Kate, "but listen. You tell Mom, and you will regret it. All your stuff will be gone—your bike, your computer and computer games, all your toys—and you'll never see any of them again."

"And your lunch will be raided every day," Analyse added. "We know people. We can arrange for things to happen."

Kate gave her a look that said maybe she had gone too far.

"I won't tell," Gavin insisted. "I promise."

Kate sighed heavily. "Give me your pinky." Gavin locked his pinky finger with Kate's and repeated his promise. "And you'll listen and do what we say. We're the leaders."

Gavin wiped his face with his sleeve. From her backpack Kate pulled a granola bar, which he wolfed down in a few seconds. Now they were three, and Gavin would be lead weight because he was so inexperienced. He knew nothing about What Is. But he was an enthusiastic traveler, they had to give him that. Hopefully, his ambition would be enough to help him keep up.

For a while, Gavin followed obediently behind the girls, but as he gained confidence, he regularly strode off ahead of them with Kate yelling at him to hold up. Their way led them through a field of grass reaching as high as their waists.

At one point, Gavin ran off ahead and disappeared around a bend in the trail. As the girls rounded the curve, the trail split in two directions, but they could not see Gavin or tell which fork he had taken. They yelled for him but there was no answer. They decided they would each take one of the forks and give a loud whoop when they found him.

Kate followed the narrow path to the right and two minutes later saw Gavin standing far off the trail in the tall grass.

"Gavin, stay there! Don't go any further." Kate gave three whoops, and within a couple of minutes Analyse had run to join her.

"I'm going to kick his little butt," Analyse said. He'd already broken his pledge.

"Over here!" Gavin shouted. Only his head and shoulders were visible above the grass as he waved to them. He was watching something. As the girls came toward him, they saw a woman leaning her back against a tree with her head bowed. Gavin shouted to try and catch the woman's attention.

"Stop it," said Kate. "We don't know who that is."

"She's in trouble," said Gavin. "Look."

The woman seemed to be holding her face in her hands, seemingly in distress, weeping uncontrollably. Kate yelled to get her attention, and the woman looked up. The three of them stepped back in horror. The woman had no face or defining features—no eyes or mouth, only a vague outline of a nose and chin. She wore a long sleeveless dress and a shawl, but her arms and hands were not visible. There was a rope around her waist that fastened her to the tree. All of a sudden, more human figures rose out of the grass like phantoms, also missing various body parts. They gazed at the young travelers.

"Welcome into our company," one woman said cheerfully, only her mouth, eyes, and ears visible.

Gavin, Kate, and Analyse immediately turned to run, but their way was blocked by other ghost-like people. The ghosts closed in and began a slow dance ritual, circling them and chanting. An acrid odour, like burning hair, rose from their captors. As the circle tightened around them, they froze. Eventually the three of them succumbed, unable to resist the hypnotic chant. Their breathing grew heavy, and they collapsed asleep in the tall grass.

When they woke, they were lying on stretchers made of tree limbs, carried in a long procession over the heads of the strangely disfigured people. Kate tried to jump down, but she could not move, paralyzed. Analyse and Gavin were being carried ahead of her. Analyse lifted her head and looked back at Kate. Her forehead was marked with a red "X." Kate rubbed her own forehead and brought down a handful of red paint. They had been branded.

The crowd stopped and lowered them to the ground, apparently taking a break. Some of them took out food items and ate. One woman held out some bread in a basket to their three captives. She smelled rancid, and her hands were missing, making the basket of bread appear suspended in midair.

Kate motioned the woman away, and Analyse turned and vomited. Their ghostly escort of twenty or so lounged around in the grass, quietly eating. Some lay back taking naps. One elderly man was missing his torso with only his ribs visible. He looked like a birdcage. Kate watched bites of food travel down in slow waves into the vacant space below the man's neck and settle in a pile where his stomach should have been. The food hung suspended like a misshapen bird in its grim cage.

Kate whispered to Analyse and Gavin, "Can you guys move? We have to get up and try to get out of here."

Gavin sobbed as they rose slowly from their stretchers. The girls had to help Gavin, one under each arm, as they stumbled back the way they'd come. But their legs could not move fast enough, as if in a nightmare.

Someone in the crowd raised the alarm, and two men, one without arms and the other with no head, started off running after them. Suddenly, there was a chorus of loud honking. Kate looked up to see a flock of geese gliding in for a raucous landing at their feet.

"Hop on! Hop on! Shadows all, shadows fall!" the geese said.

Without waiting for a response, three geese quickly wiggled their way under the knees of Gavin, Analyse, and Kate, causing them to fall forward onto the backs of three other geese for their double goose transport. Gavin and Analyse screamed.

"Just wrap your arms around their necks and hold on!" Kate yelled as they lifted off the ground. They looked down at their would be captors, who watched them go.

They flew back in the direction of Singing Meadow, undoing two hours of walking in a matter of minutes. There below them was Rocky Mound. A small group of animals was assembled, watching them as they approached. On one of the large rocks a bear was standing on his hind legs. The flock of geese and their three travelers passed over and circled gracefully back for a landing as the geese raised a chorus.

> *Day is closing, evening is nigh.*
> *Winged on the wind and watched on high,*
> *our fearless companions, kingdom friends,*
> *rescued on time from the Shadows' end.*

Waiting on Rocky Mound was Corvus with a large company of his crow friends. Also, Budsley was there and three other beavers, a couple of kingfishers, and two bears. Two eagles were perched on the largest rock, facing in opposite directions, as if on watch, and in the background stood numerous deer, looking shy and unaccustomed to large gatherings. Analyse, Gavin, and Kate looked in sheer amazement.

"How did you know we were in trouble?" Kate said.

"I made sure someone was watching," Corvus said, nodding toward the eagles. "No better eyes in the Kingdom. No one goes on an important quest without the need of a rescue mission now and then." The geese roared their agreement. "Some situations are beyond our control."

"First we were there . . . " stuttered Analyse, "and suddenly . . . we were up in the sky and . . . " She was still trying to catch her breath.

The bears roared with laughter, and the beavers slapped their tails.

"And who have we here?" Corvus inquired, "Another one along on the journey?"

"Oh," said Kate, "this is my brother."

"Brother. Welcome."

Gavin was standing speechless, bewildered at the company of animals around him. It was clear he did not hear any of them speaking.

"What were those . . . those human creatures we ran into?" Analyse asked.

Before Corvus could answer, the deer came forward dragging several travois, loaded with a vast assortment of food, including mussels and clams from the shore, and trout from Budsley Pond. There was a salad of stinging nettles along with a lush pile of berries, and there were roots of more kinds than they could have imagined, all cleaned and chopped to bite size.

A bear motioned for Kate to take a seat on her favorite rock as the deer pulled the travois to a stop in front of her. The geese started a rousing song, which must have been their version of "Happy Birthday."

Once a fair day, a little girl was born,
to the Kingdom chair she now is borne.
Now feast and cheer one and all,
and bend your ear to this birthday call.

On the final note the animals let out a loud call, each in his or her own unique voice, which strained the ear. They had arranged a birthday party!

"Who told you . . . " Kate began.

"I have my sources," Corvus said.

"A little birdie told you?"

"You're catching on."

Kate had never felt so honored. The birthday meal was spread. The bears were first to pounce. They went immediately for the berries, which they mostly finished before anyone else could get to them, and then moved on to the trout. The deer held back in disgust at the bears' total lack of manners before slowly moving in on the stinging nettle salad. The beavers went for the rich variety of roots. And the crows were a row of bobbing heads, pecking at the clams in a cacophony of clicking beaks against shells like a line of castanet players in a band.

When it appeared the food was nearly gone, Budsley approached, followed by a deer with a rope in her mouth. She pulled a little red wagon. In the wagon was a partially eaten birthday cake with five candles and the lettering on the cake still intact. It said, "Happy Birthday Chad."

Kate stared quizzically. "Chad?"

"A team effort," Corvus said. "Let's say we rescued it and leave it at that."

Analyse and Kate laughed hysterically until their stomachs hurt.

"At the count of three, everyone dive in," Budsley instructed. "And no arguing." All the animals, except for the bears who were already asleep, gawked uncertainly at the cake. Out of respect, they each had a mouthful before being overcome by a dizzying sugar rush, unaccustomed as they were to triple-layer chocolate cake with chocolate frosting.

When the cake was finished, they all lay virtually unconscious, uttering low indistinguishable sounds along with lots of burping.

Kate, Analyse, and Gavin returned to Wild Rose Passage just as daylight was fading in the Kingdom of What Is. When they emerged on the other side, it was still mid day. Kate and Analyse had ten minutes to show up at Brody's detention room.

"Those animals—they're so smart," Gavin said excitedly as they made their way back to school. "It seemed like they were trying to talk to us, and that goose ride . . . was that real?"

"Well," said Analyse, "what's that?"

Gavin looked down and pulled a goose feather from his shirt.

Chapter 9

The Ancients

Analyse came home with Kate after school for her birthday. Kate's mom had created a birthday banner and draped it across the dining room. There were also thirteen balloons with the number "13" printed on them for the occasion, strategically hung to give the house a balance of color. It was a little over the top, but Kate gave her mom a long hug of appreciation for the gesture.

Her mom made her a cake with "Happy Birthday Kate" on it. The girls laughed, remembering the cake stolen from some kid named Chad, going into stitches so that her candles had almost completely melted before Kate could blow them out. She had to assure her mom that their laughter had nothing to do with the cake. Though they were not really hungry for more cake, they each took a small piece and went up to bed early so they could talk.

Kate's only birthday request had been for Analyse to stay for a sleepover. It gave them a chance to reflect and strategize.

They went over all they'd done so far in What Is and recorded it in Kate's journal. They turned to the map and added the places they'd been and paths they'd taken, both on purpose and by mistake. The map was expanding as their knowledge of the Kingdom was expanding. They agreed the journal would stay with Kate at all times from now on so no sticky fingers could get hold of it.

"And the next time, we'll leave for the woods when we're sure Gavin doesn't know we're going," Analyse said.

"And make sure we bring more water this time. It was so hot, I was sweating in five minutes."

The next day was Saturday, and the girls didn't wake up until ten o'clock when they heard people outside. Analyse jumped up and peeked through her curtains. Gavin was talking to Nolan in front of the house.

"Guess who's here, it's Nolan," she said. "Kate, he's in love with you!"

"No he's not, he's my friend, that's it."

The next thing they heard was Gavin calling Kate to come outside. The girls put on slippers, pulled their hoodies on over their pajamas, and sat out on the front steps.

"Happy birthday," Nolan said shyly, "yesterday."

"Thanks," Kate said, her eyes searching for the present he'd promised to bring.

"Let's hang out in the park," Nolan said.

The girls went in to get their shoes on and pull on some pants, and walked out the front gate with Nolan.

"Gavin, you're staying," ordered Kate over her shoulder.

They sat slowly rocking on swings in the playground. The morning was chilly but sunny, and they were in a relaxed mood. Nolan was taking selfies with his phone of him and the girls. They made silly small talk, told jokes, and complained loudly about the science projects they had to present—two before Christmas!

Nolan said he wanted to give Kate her birthday present, so the two of them left Analyse and wandered off for a short walk.

Later on, after Nolan had left, Analyse asked her, "So what did he give you?"

"Nothing," Kate said nervously.

"Yes he did. What?"

"He wanted to give me a ring, and I told him no, I just wanted him to be my friend, so I didn't take it. I said, like I'm only thirteen, and he goes, well I'm going to be fourteen in January, but I still said no. He said he was cool with it." Then she admitted quietly, "We kissed once this summer," letting her hair drape over her face.

"You kissed? You lied! You told me you didn't."

"Only once, that was it. And it was nothing."

"What did it feel like?"

"I don't know. Wet and tickly, I guess. It's past. I'm just not interested now."

With that, she suddenly grabbed Analyse by the hand, ran to the house, and snuck in through the back door while Gavin and Mom were out front playing with Norbert. The girls crept quietly up the stairs, grabbed their packs from Kate's room, glanced back to make sure no one saw them leaving the house, and raced again out the back door. They were at the park in seconds. The maple trees glowed golden above them as they ran, leaves falling like shimmering flames. They could hardly keep from screaming with excitement.

Hunkered down at Wild Rose Passage, they made sure Gavin or no one else saw them come. Pushing aside the long rose stems, they quickly ducked in.

They passed by the beaver pond, through the meadow to its farthest end, and up the hill to Rocky Mound. They felt energetic and made no stops, wanting to complete what they had started last time. In less than two hours they again reached the fork where Gavin had gone missing. This time they took the fork to the left and walked another hour before pausing to catch their breath.

Near the path, a goat stood staring at them. It bleated loudly, which made them jump.

"What's that?" Kate asked.

"A goat, dummy."

"No, that," Kate pointed.

Analyse pushed up her glasses and squinted. Well off the path, beyond the goat, was a dome shaped pile of debris near a grove of trees. It was low to the ground, well camouflaged and tucked along the tree line. It would have easily been missed if they had not stopped.

"Let's have a look," Kate said, taking several steps off the trail.

"Kate, don't." But her warning went unheeded as Kate walked up to within a few feet of the strange structure. A thin line of smoke was rising from the dome.

"Holy guacamole, it's a house!" said Analyse.

Kate was about to rush forward when Analyse said, "We don't know who or what's in there."

Kate charged ahead. The house was actually a large round mound of earth with shrubs growing over it. On one side of the mound was a wall several feet high with two windows and a door. Kate glanced through the window and knocked but no one seemed to be home.

Analyse, who had climbed halfway up the dome, called down, "It's like one of those earth houses, half underground. Look at this." She held up a small glass bowl. "They've got these bowls lying upside down all over the mound. Weird."

Kate tried the door and it swung open. She stepped in.

"Hello?" she said, looking into a space so dark she could not make out its shape or size. As her eyes adjusted, she was surprised to notice there was more than adequate light to see clearly. The large dome ceiling was perforated with holes, which let light in from the outside. That must be what those glass bowls are for, Kate thought. Cool. Little sky lights.

The interior was divided into rooms. The large front room Kate stood in extended the length of the house. It had a stone floor and a stone fireplace against one wall, where a weak flame flickered. The fireplace was bracketed by two couches cut out of large logs that were covered with blankets. At the opposite end of the room was a kitchen with a wood-burning stove, a table and four chairs, and a counter along the entire wall. It's half ancient and half Star Wars, Kate thought. On the table four plates and cups were set out. She picked up a cup. It was warm.

Before leaving, she grabbed a couple of plums and a chunk of bread off the counter and stuffed them into her pockets. She stopped outside the door to let their eyes readjust to daylight. When she regained focus, she fell back. In front of her was not her friend Analyse, as she'd expected, but a woman and a bearded man crouching on the top step, with two kids standing behind them. The oldest kid was a boy about Gavin's age. They all stared at her for a moment.

"We saw you on the trail," the man said. "Where did your friend go?"

Kate glanced around. Analyse was gone.

"Where are your parents?" the woman asked.

"At home," Kate answered, shaking.

"Well, you're not from very far away, or you wouldn't have come alone," the man said.

"We don't want any trouble, we're good neighbors," Kate said without really thinking. She attempted to cover her bulging pockets with her hands.

The man and woman glanced at each other. Then the woman reached into a satchel hanging from her shoulder and pulled out more plums. "Here," she said. "Try one of these. They're much fresher than those old ones you've got there."

Kate was too embarrassed to accept them.

"Come inside," the woman said. "For now you belong with us." She smiled and pointed back toward the grove. "Is that your friend there?"

A bespectacled red-haired girl peeked out from behind a tree. The owners of the house motioned for her to follow them inside, where the woman ladled some kind of stew for them while the man cut two large pieces of bread off a loaf.

"I'm sorry about the plums," Kate said. "I took this bread too." She held out the evidence.

"Don't be sorry, keep them," said the man. "They are not ours to hoard but a gift." The man said it as a proverb, as if reminding the girls of something they ought not to have forgotten. "The King and Queen gave us the land. And the land gave us this."

He held up a chunk of bread and closed his eyes. "*Chaova*!" he said, which sounded like a blessing and an invitation to eat.

The man held his arms out wide to include everyone in the house and those beyond. "It's royal land and we're its keepers," he said. "The King gives us the land and tools, we help it grow—"

"Okay, enough with the lecture," the woman said. "I'm sure they've heard it."

The two kids, whom their mom introduced as Yochan and Julia, joined them at the table, and instantly the family started a boisterous song:

Rumpity rum pum, hey ho!
Good cheer to the King
and the rain to make it grow!
Rumpity rum pum, hey ho!
From the land to the kettle
and down it goes!
Hey ho! Rumpity rum pum!
Curse the old Vurm!
And we all say Yum!

"And kick him in the bum!" added little Julia with a wide grin.

The family took a big first bite all together as if placing an exclamation point on the last line of the song. Kate and Analyse were too hungry to ask what the stew was and took more of everything. It was beyond their best dreams to find someone who would welcome them so generously into their home.

The man introduced himself as Grover. "Keeper of the grove," he explained.

"And I'm Aster," said the woman. She'd taken the name when she realized how much she loved the night sky. The girls looked at the ceiling and understood. It was like a planetarium, with the holes in the dome creating stars and planets. "I can see the stars all day," Aster said. "When the haze in the sky is too thick, I can always see the world in here the way it is supposed to be."

Kate remembered the pages with star charts that the stranger had ripped out of her textbook at the cave. "Do people around here like the stars?"

"Oh yes," said Aster, "they're very important, especially in these dark times. They show us the way, when the skies are clear. The stars and planets can even prophesy the future if you know how to read them. But mostly they remind us the King and Queen are still in control. That's why Vurmis has tried so hard to block them out with his awful smog, you know? He hopes we'll lose our way."

"Prophesy?" Kate asked.

"A time is coming of deep sorrow and great happiness," Aster said confidently. "That much has been made plain."

"I think we saw the deep sorrow already," Analyse said, "at the Great Gorge."

Their hosts were startled to hear her mention the Great Gorge and wondered why they had gone there. The girls told them about their adventure there, how they'd come upon it unexpectedly, and what they'd seen, things Grover and Aster already knew but were surprised to hear from two young girls.

"It looked so scary and sad," Kate said.

"A sorrow is coming deeper than the Great Gorge or the Plague, much deeper than all other sorrows."

"And the great happiness?" Kate asked.

"Yes, great happiness as well. Sorrow and happiness will meet together."

"Like thorns on roses?" asked Analyse.

Aster thought. "Well, yes. Perhaps like thorns on roses."

Grover interrupted. "We'll talk more in the morning when our minds are fresh. It's not good to go to sleep with dark thoughts."

Kate looked over at Analyse. They were apparently spending the night.

"Thank you for dinner," the girls said. "Delicious."

"It's rabbit, herbs, and nettles," Aster said.

The girls were glad they hadn't asked before eating it. Stewed rabbit was not on their shortlist of delicacies they wanted to try, even in a tight spot.

Kate quickly interjected one more question. "Do the animals . . . you know . . . talk to you?"

"Yes, they do. If you have the ears to hear them, you'll hear them," Grover said as Kate nodded. "And we'd be much the poorer for not paying attention."

Kate looked down into her bowl.

"Ah. You're wondering about the rabbit we stewed," Grover said. "You're a sensitive soul, that's a great treasure." He explained like a wise, kind teacher, "It isn't easy to take the life of something you respect dearly and rely on for wisdom, then simply to eat it. Rabbits and goats don't want to die any more than any of us, but they do know about sacrifice, perhaps more than we do. It's the way of the land, the way of the Kingdom, but it's important we never take their sacrifices for granted . . . as something they owe us. Thankfulness—that's the important thing—thanks to the rabbit, to the land, and to the King and Queen. The same for the roots and herbs. They give their lives too, right?"

Kate said, "I never thought of it like that. Poor potatoes."

Grover's red beard danced as he delighted in Kate's wit and in the simple wonder of the truths he obviously loved talking about.

Aster interjected, "You'll probably hear him say the same things a few more times while you're here. But you'll notice," she added as she pulled the bread plate away from Grover's reach and slapped his hand, "he forgot the part about taking from the land only as much as you need."

"Story time!" Yochan reminded his dad.

They moved to the sofas by the fireplace as Grover handed around large mugs of a sweet drink like liquid yogurt. Grover took a deep breath and started in on a story, the kids listening intently.

"Okay!" Grover rubbed his hands together. "Let's see . . . The King and Queen were holding a great feast—a harvest feast—at the home of a very prosperous farmer and his wife. Their home was chosen because it had a large well—the only well in the area with enough good water for the hundreds of guests who were to come to the feast.

"It had been a dry year and some farmers had been short of water for their animals and gardens. So this feast would be a very special treat for many.

"To be chosen by the royal family as the place for the harvest feast, of course, was a great honor. But the farmer and his wife were concerned. If they had to draw water for everyone at the feast, and use more for cleaning up, what would be left for themselves and their livestock? Their well would easily run dry.

"So to be safe, before the feast, the farmer drew enough water from the well to fill six barrels and hid these barrels in the woods behind the barn. He reasoned that this would get him through another drought, if necessary. For good measure, he also tied up three goats in the woods to ensure they would have meat through the winter.

"Well, over three hundred guests arrived. People brought produce from their homes—vegetables of every kind, bread, chickens, and several goats. For some, it was all that they had. The feast was spread, music was played, and everyone ate until they were full and then ate some more and there was still food left over. People were the happiest they had been for that entire year. Old acquaintances and friendships were renewed. Grievances were settled. And interestingly, in spite of the very dry year it had been, there was water enough to drink for everyone and even enough to clean up with. A few even took much needed baths. It was everything the King and Queen had wanted it to be.

"After the last guest had gone home, as the King and Queen were thanking the farmer and his wife for hosting the feast, they heard a loud bleating from the woods behind the barn. Then there were several loud splashes. The farmer's goats had broken free, and out of thirst they had knocked over the barrels of water.

"The King and Queen were distressed. 'Didn't we give you the land and the water and these goats? Yet, you've held these back from your guests for this great celebration. Did you fear you would go thirsty and hungry so that you had to keep these for yourselves?'

"That winter was a harsh one—cold and dry. The water and the goats were enough for the farmer and his wife to survive. But they could not drink or eat because of the weight of guilt they carried. They grew sick and their goats died of neglect.

"Their neighbors and friends came, bringing what water and food they had. Finally, after repeated urging, the couple began to eat and drink, a little at a time until slowly, and through many tears, they managed to regain their strength, and lived."

The story made Kate's skin tingle. Everyone was quiet for several minutes. The kids were dozing off.

Finally Kate asked, "Did that really happen?"

Grover look at Aster. "Yes, it did," Aster said.

"One more," Yochan said, suddenly rousing from half-sleep.

They heard hooting noises from outside.

"The owls are calling," said Aster. "That means time for bed, kids, come on." The kids dragged themselves away to bed. Aster showed the girls a room, where there were two thick mats laid out on the floor, not like their beds back home but very comfortable. They pulled large blankets over themselves.

"Analyse," Kate whispered as the house went quiet.

"What?"

"That Grover is loqua—What was that word that means 'likes talking'?"

"Loquacious. Yeah, I like him."

"These people are, like, the best I've ever met. They must be the Ancients Corvus was talking about. So, do you trust them?" Kate asked.

"I trust anybody who can make their house look like a planetarium. So cool. Aster's a dreamer, eh?"

The girls lay admiring the "stars" in the ceiling, whose glow was slowly fading as darkness fell. The next thing Kate said landed on deaf ears. Analyse had already fallen asleep.

When Aster was showing them into their room, Kate had poked her head around one corner and noticed a short passage with steps that led down to something like a cellar door.

She first listened for signs of people still awake before creeping out of the room and taking the stairs. At the bottom, she slowly opened the door. A strong musty smell greeted her. In the dimness she saw a long, narrow room. Along the walls were shelves with hundreds of old books.

She took one down and flipped through its pages. Dust rose from the book, causing her to sneeze. Even in the poor light she could tell the book in her hand was not English. Some pages had maps. Others had sketches of old style weapons. This was an archive of some kind. She was about to remove another book when she heard footsteps behind her. Someone was coming down the stairs.

Chapter 10

Storms, Stars, and Stories

"It's my dad's library." It was Yochan. "You can read those, but he wouldn't like it if you were in here without asking."

"I was just . . . " Kate stammered, "I was just curious. Sorry."

She exited as Yochan closed the door and inserted a key in the lock, followed by a loud click. He said, "Don't worry, I won't tell."

In the middle of the night the girls were woken by pounding that sounded like a herd of horses running over the dome above them. It went on and on, accompanied by a howling wind that grew louder and more intense. They crawled deeper under their blankets and covered their ears. Glass broke and fell from the ceiling.

"What's going on?" Analyse screamed.

The pounding and wind finally stopped as suddenly as it had begun. A couple of balls of ice lay on the floor—it was a hail storm. One of the small skylights had broken out, and glass sat in a puddle of water. They lay awake, bracing themselves for another barrage. The air had cooled considerably from the storm, but within minutes, the temperature rose again, so high the girls were in a sweat and had to shed their blankets. It was completely dark and silent, and they felt the sensation of a large hand pushing them down in their beds.

"What are we doing here?" Analyse sobbed.

Kate wondered how any place could be such a strange mix of beauty and dread. This family was lovely and awesome, but at the moment the evil in this land seemed overwhelming. She worried that in spite of their urgency to meet the King and Queen, they might find the leaders of this fair land were not powerful enough to stop Vurmis and end the Plague. The thought gave her a sudden chill.

In the morning they heard movement in the house. They went to the large front room. Aster was entering with an armful of potatoes, carrots, and a few other vegetables they didn't recognize.

"Grover's looking after the trees," Aster said, putting out some cake rounds. Next to the cake was a plate of dried fish and seaweed. "Bad storms usually mean lots of tree damage in the grove . . . and to my ceiling lights . . . it will be a long day. If the limbs build up on the ground, eventually a fire could set the whole grove ablaze. The storms are getting more violent." She rambled on and burst out, "*Shakrum* Vurmis," which sounded like some kind of curse.

Grover came in with twigs hanging from his beard. Kate searched his face. If he knew of her sneaking into his library last night, he didn't show it.

The girls were full of questions that had been churning inside them.

"Have you ever visited the King and Queen?" Kate asked outright.

"We don't really need to visit them," said Aster. "They come to us. We see one or the other in this area now and then. Have you never seen them in your area?"

"They come here?" Kate asked, surprised. This didn't fit with her image of royalty hanging out in castles, sending out messengers, and never leaving except on important business.

"Of course," said Aster. "Sometimes just one of them comes—the King, the Queen, or the Prince, or sometimes all three arrive together. Almost always unannounced."

Little Julia touted, "Prince Servan gave me a ride on his shoulders!"

"They have a son?"

"You didn't know?" Aster asked puzzled. "I suppose it's not very widely known because he is still young—a little older than you maybe although his actual age is a mystery. And many have grown so tired of the Plague they've lost interest in the royal family—they've lost faith that the royals can do anything about it. It's entirely possible the royal family has visited your town and no one knew it because they didn't recognize them. Many don't expect to see royalty anymore, so they wouldn't see them even if they were right in front of them."

"But why do they come here?" Analyse asked.

"Well, because. It's their land after all . . . their people . . . and they do care about what's happening."

Grover took a swallow of his drink and wrinkled his brow. "Where are you from?"

"Shelby," Kate answered without thinking that these people had probably never heard of such a place.

"Shall Be . . . Shall Be . . . " Grover turned the name over in his mind. "Never heard of it, but it's a good name, I like it. It's hopeful."

"It's far away," Kate tried to clarify.

"So, you are . . . on a quest, a very long and daring quest, to meet the King and Queen," Grover said, trying to summarize what he'd learned from them."

"Right," said Kate.

"But you don't exactly know how to get there."

"Right. And we're looking for wise guides along the way," Kate said, remembering what Corvus had told them.

"Hmm." Grover stroked his beard. "We can't go with you, but we can help."

Grover explained the route and warned them of some of the difficulties they should expect, leaning on his knowledge of the history of the Kingdom and the area. "Most people think Grod Vurmis is just a trouble-maker who's making life difficult. But he is more than just irritating. He's cunning. And he's continuing what his father Grod Forza started, only worse, by taking over the Great Gorge. The more he takes, the more he wants . . . the land, the life in it . . . and our lives."

"The Plague," Analyse said.

"Yes, the sickness he spreads all over the land, in the rivers, in the cities . . . it's everywhere. These odd storms like last night are an awful part of it. That's why we built this house—to be partially underground. It's better protection from storms, and from the unbearable heat too. But, it's hard to find a perfect home in these times."

"This home feels perfect to me," Kate said.

"Grod Forza was no different from anyone else in a way—he wanted a perfect home. But he also wanted an entire kingdom, separate from everyone else except for those who wanted to join him. His son Vurmis has bigger ideas, much more sinister. Rather than set up a separate kingdom, he aims to take over the entire Kingdom from Athar and Sapienta. The Great Gorge you saw—that's his stronghold, and it's where people end up if they give in to him."

"We never would," Analyse said.

"You never would willingly, but you might if you were deceived into it. As quickly as you said 'no, not me,' you could be under his control and part of his plan," he said with a grave sincerity in his eyes.

Kate and Analyse told him about their encounter with the ghost-like people the day before.

"Shadows," Aster called from the other end of the room. "Steer clear of them, they can't be trusted."

Grover said, "Shadows—the Dreglings who have been with Vurmis the longest."

"Dreglings?"

"Yes, all the followers of Vurmis. You probably have Dreglings living right in Shall Be and don't even know it. They've infiltrated everywhere. Over time under Vurmis's influence, Dreglings slowly fade to nothing. With each passing day their bodies disappear until they are almost entirely gone, and they are only shadows of what they once were. Sometimes, only the keen eye can make out their form—or pick them out of a crowd if they have not yet turned to Shadows. The worst part is not the losing of their bodies but completely forgetting who they are."

Kate and Analyse went pale as Grover continued explaining how Dreglings were once common citizens who fell in with Vurmis. They first thought they were becoming part of a new kingdom with a glorious future but were now among the disappearing and the disappeared. "Vurmis promises them a new life with everything they need. But they actually become slaves, forced into carrying out his plans to take over the Kingdom. Most don't even realize they've been conned."

"So it's not their fault then?" Kate asked. "They've been tricked."

"Tricked or simply captured, as you almost were," Grover said.

"But they have a choice," Aster clarified. "To stay or run. As you did. So it actually *is* their fault."

"It's not that simple," Grover argued. "Running isn't always an option when you're a slave."

"They're responsible for falling for him," Aster countered firmly and walked away.

Aster and Grover went quiet. This was apparently an ongoing debate—about how much Dreglings were at fault or how much they were victims. It obviously wasn't going to be settled in one sitting.

"Dad," Yochan interrupted, "show them your library."

Kate took a bite of dried fish, trying to avoid Grover's eyes. Analyse glanced around, looking for a library.

"You have a library?" Analyse asked.

"Yes, a few of us have them. I wouldn't show it to just anyone, but I trust you," he said, smiling and brushing crumbs from his hands.

He showed them down the stairs to the room Kate had found the night before and unlocked the door. With the help of the skylights Kate saw clearly what she could only vaguely make out the night before. Most of the books were from another era. They were stacked on shelves five high on either side of the long room.

Grover pushed aside some broken glass with his foot, took down a few books that had been soaked by the storm, and put them to one side.

"The real stories are here, and some in other libraries. Together they make up the royal story," Grover explained.

"Royal story?" Kate asked.

"Of what has been, what is, and what will be. Some libraries have been ransacked, books stolen. Vurmis's plan is to take the old stories . . . as well as some of the old storytellers. He's rewriting everything, you see, with himself as the main character. I got my hands on a couple of his books from some peddlers. He simply revises and twists the old stories and replaces their covers—disgusting. He reproduces them by the hundreds. How people can fall for it is beyond me. I guess because they just don't know the real stories. A few storytellers have already gone over to him, but those who remain loyal are trying to preserve the Kingdom stories."

"Are you a storyteller?" Kate asked.

"One of several. We come together regularly—to retell the stories and keep them alive, and to avoid inaccuracies. To make sure we're all on the same page, if you get my meaning. A minor variation here or there in the telling of a story is not the end of the world. But a mistake that changes the story's meaning, something that changes the spirit of a story—that would be unacceptable.

"We are also copying some of the rarest books, translating others, and storing them in a safe place. Only the royal family and a couple of us know where. The best and safest place to store them is right here." Grover patted his chest. "If Vurmis destroys all our books, the stories won't die if we have them in our hearts, right? And if our hearts fail us, as they sometimes do, the true stories will not die if we have them in books." He looked gravely at the girls. "And if we lose heart and lose the books, well . . . we're finished, and the Kingdom is Vurmis's."

Grover continued to pull down various volumes, checking them for water damage, talking to them as if they were his beloved children.

"So you see, storytelling and story keeping is serious business. We wouldn't do it if we didn't understand the greater purpose. And we love stories!" he added with a giddy laugh, as if story-telling was the greatest job anyone could ever ask for.

Kate looked down the rows of books. "That's a lot of stories to keep track of."

"And we have our whole lives to learn them, copy them, and pass them on! And my kids after me will do the same if they love the stories as much as I do." Grover gently pulled out a book and opened it with tender affection. "This is one of Aster's favorites." Kate saw that it was full of star charts. The girls felt dwarfed by the rows and rows of books.

"It's like we're in a forest of books!" Analyse said.

"Indeed, a forest in book form, well done." Grover threw his head back and his beard shook as he laughed with sheer pleasure. "From the trees to the library, a worthy investment. I'm a keeper of two groves! Thank you for that."

Analyse was pulling on a book that stuck out slightly from its place on the shelf.

"Ah!" Grover said. "You have good taste."

Analyse read the title, *The Battle of Yochan Creek,* and handed it to Grover, who held out the book and gazed at it. "An old friend! The very battle my son was named after. And I'd love to share it with you, but you have a journey ahead of you, don't you, possibly battles too . . . and you'll be adding your own stories to the ones here, I'm sure. Giving me much more work to do."

He stroked his beard and waited for the girls to ask him to read a few pages. When they didn't respond, he said finally, "Ah, why not! What's the harm in just a few pages before you have to leave?"

Back in the living room, Grover said, "Before we get to the good part, we need to read the not so good part."

The story began with the assault on the castle and the beginnings of the Great Rebellion under Grod Forza against King Athar and Queen Sapienta. Forza took one thousand people with him to begin a new kingdom beyond the mountains to the east, splitting families, dividing brother from brother, friend from friend, and they never saw each other again.

The girls remembered the carvings they found in the rocks at the Great Gorge and asked Grover about them.

"The etchings," Grover said, "they're a recent strategy of Vurmis. As he rewrites the old stories and turns them upside down, he also carves his stories in pictures everywhere. They're his propaganda. That way, if people read his stories and see his pictures often enough, they'll start to believe them rather than the old stories. If he ever discovered my library, he'd take the most valuable books and destroy the rest."

"But he couldn't just fool everyone that easily," Kate protested.

"You would think not. But people have grown lazy and dull, so they are easily fooled."

"So you and your family are the Ancients?" Analyse wanted to confirm.

"One family among many. We're called Ancients because we're loyal to the royal family and the traditions, but we're really no more special than you or anyone else."

"Why can't the King and Queen do something about Vurmis?" Kate asked.

"They are, little by little, involving every means they can. And they have a secret plan that will be definitive."

"Secret plan?"

"Which they might share with you if you were among those to help carry it out," Grover said.

Aster, who had been patiently listening, said, "I'm glad you found us. Now I understand what the stars have been saying. You may be the ones foretold."

Kate and Analyse looked at each other.

"Aries has been brighter than usual this year, trying to call attention to something. You know the story about the talking ram with a golden fleece—Aries? He carries the two siblings away from home through the sky to help them escape sure death by sacrifice."

Kate's throat tightened. She thought of the Shadows and their rescue ride, not on a talking ram, no, but on talking geese. "So what happens?" Kate asked anxiously.

"Well, on the long flight, one of the siblings falls tragically into the sea, while the other is flown to safety in a new land. Then the ram is sacrificed, leaving its golden fleece, and the Kingdom prospers. What the stars prophesy does not always happen exactly like it does in the story, or how we think it should. Sometimes there's what we call a 'slight departure' from the stars' prophesy or an 'unexpected disruption.'"

"So . . . " Analyse said, "what part of the story is going to happen for sure?"

"We won't know until it happens," said Aster matter-of-factly. Seeing the worried expressions on the girls' faces, she added, "The prophesies never give us all the details, and for good reason. Why would we try if we knew exactly what was going to happen to us? What fun would that be? The stories of the stars are there to guide and encourage you, and the rest is left to your wisdom and choices along the way. You fill in the details."

The girls would have been frightened had it not been for Aster's sincerity and calmness.

Their hosts supplied the girls with some fresh water, deer jerky, and fresh bread for the trek. Aster also made sure they had blankets, which they tied to their packs, should they need to spend a night or two under the stars. The days were plenty warm, but the nights could get cold. The family walked with them to the main trail.

"Stay to the path," Grover said, "with your eyes to the palace. Who knows, you may even meet the royal family before you get there."

The girls looked over the grasslands gleaming in the sunrise. To their right, the land rose eastward to the mountains. To the left, the land sloped gently down westward to the ocean.

"You can smell the sea this morning," Aster said. "It's a good omen."

Grover told the girls they would come to a fork in the trail. They were to follow the path going westward to the sea. The other direction east would likely lead them into encounters with Dreglings.

He explained they would come to a fishing village on the coast called Gulls Landing, a full day's journey. "It's at the mouth of the River Royal. When you reach it, look for a boat builder named Bowman. He's my cousin, a good man. If he can't take you up the river to the palace himself, he'll find someone who can."

Aster said, "When you meet people on the way, tell them, 'We come in the name of the King.' If the person returns the same greeting, you'll know you're in good hands."

"What if they're faking it?" Analyse said.

"No one can say those words while looking you in the eye," Grover said. "If they're lying, they'll look away, or you might feel a trembling in their handshake. Be alert."

As they set off, the girls felt both grateful for their new friends and sad at leaving them. They turned to see Yochan and Julia jumping up and down, yelling to them, and waving good-bye.

Chapter 11

Unexpected Company

Around them the tall grass waved in the morning breeze, which carried a scent of brine from the west. They were excited. The beauty of the land and of people like Aster and Grover were proof their quest was right. Still, they were wary as their eyes scanned the landscape around them for any signs of Dreglings. They had already seen and heard enough of Vurmis's work not to be cautious.

They were grateful Gavin was not with them. It was much safer without him making dumb moves and saying the wrong thing at the wrong time. He would never know they'd gone because they would be back before he had time to wonder where they were.

When they reached the junction Grover told them about, they took the left fork, which would take them to Gulls Landing on the sea at the mouth of the River Royal. Walking became easier on a gradual downhill slope, and the trail was wider with two well-worn ruts where wheels had frequently passed over. The air had an intoxicating fresh aroma that gave them such energy they could hardly keep themselves from running. Analyse jumped up onto a boulder along the trail.

"Kate, I can see the ocean! It's turquoise!"

The ocean was a thin line on the horizon. As they took it in, they tried a few bites of deer jerky and roots. The bitterness of the roots convinced them to try grinding them up first and mixing the pulp in water as a drink. This made the roots more bearable and also made them feel full. A short distance from the trail, they noticed a patch of golden yellow berries. Analyse went to pick some.

"Wait," Kate said, "we don't know if those are edible."

"They are quite edible," a voice said from the berry bushes. A young man looked up from a basket he was filling and threw a couple of the berries into his mouth. "You're off to the Valley of Royals, I presume." His voice was soft and gentle.

"Yes," said Kate.

The man waved for them to come and held out his basket of wild berries.

"Here, take some. It's a long journey."

They eagerly took several, ate them, and took some more.

"Currants," the man said. "Have as many as you like, there's thousands. Where do you come from?"

Kate held out her hand to the south.

"Thanks for the berries," Analyse said, blushing at the kindness of the young man. "Do you want to join us?" she asked nervously, catching a berry that dropped from her hand.

Kate gave her a poke in the back to tell her to stop flirting.

The man laughed appreciatively but declined her invitation. "Thank you, but my business is here. Maybe you would care to join me for some lunch? I promise you, these berries taste much better in a pie."

"Sure," Analyse said immediately and began following him toward a house behind the berry patch. Analyse pulled Kate along by the arm.

"Stop it!" Kate hissed. "We don't know this guy."

"He could be the Prince," Analyse protested. "Don't be so skeptical. Would you rather have roots or a chance at a real lunch?"

"A chance for you to flirt." Kate jerked her hand away from Analyse.

"Never mind your friend there, all the more lunch for the two of us then," said the young man with a smile, holding out his had to Analyse.

They were interrupted by a rumbling of wheels and horse hooves back on the trail, followed by a loud whistle. It was an old man driving a horse and cart with a load of wood.

"I go in the name of the King!" the old man shouted in a gravelly voice.

The girls suddenly remembered the greeting—they'd forgotten to use it with this young man.

"Back off, Dregling!" yelled the man on the cart.

The young man with the berries grabbed Analyse's hand and pulled her toward him. She screamed, feeling this gentle man turn suddenly forceful. She struggled to free herself. She fell and he began dragging her. Out of nowhere, a wooden pole came down hard on the young man's shoulder.

He fell to the ground groaning. One of his legs came exposed, and the girls noticed it was as translucent as glass, as though it could break with the slightest effort. He got up holding his shoulder and stumbled toward his house.

"Sweetness and light, ye bold fool! Be gone with ye!" the old man shouted, raising the pole, his eyes blazing. He growled like a hoarse bear, revealing a mouth of missing teeth. "Ye won't be takin' us for idiots and fallin' for your berry pie, ye Vurmis vermin!" He spat to the ground.

When the young man had gone, the old man caught his breath and brushed himself off as if ridding himself of a spider.

"I see the Dregling had other plans for ye," he said. "He's tried it many times before and many times succeeded. He'd have taken ye into his house for pie, and once he got ye fallin' for him, he'd have led ye off on a berry huntin' expedition to the Great Gorge never to be seen again. Ye wouldn't be the first to fall for it."

There was the clomping of horse's hooves again from up the trail.

"Ah, my wife and our wayward passengers," said the old man.

Down the path came a horse and cart driven by an elderly lady stooping over the reins. Next to her sat two boys, haggard and dirty, one older than the other. The man explained that they had found them near the Great Gorge while collecting wood.

"No . . . no!" Kate screamed and covered her mouth. There were Gavin and Nolan. Tired and confused, the boys stared stupidly at the girls, and the girls stared back in shock.

"Get aboard with the old man there," the woman told the girls. "We'll take you all as far as our house."

The girls climbed onto the man's cart. Kate buried her face in her hands, wondering what to do with this unexpected, unfortunate turn of events, while Analyse sat red with anger.

"My little brother, how could they even dare?" Kate muttered.

The old man sent up more curses on the Dregling as they rode on. "Be doomed to damnation, all of ye who choose to cast in yer lot with Vurmis!"

The woman driving the boys chanted as if warding off evil spirits, "To the Gorge, to the Gorge, we'll have none of your phony porridge."

The old man grumbled, "Supposed to love them, I know, but they rankle me!" He sniffed and spat a large gob to the ground.

When they reached the old couple's home, Kate, Analyse, Gavin, and Nolan were invited in for a hot lunch. They were so hungry they ate without talking, each lost in his or her private thoughts, trying to watch their manners and not start a fight. It was mid-day and, in spite of the couple's kind offers to stay, the girls desperately wanted to try to reach the sea while it was still light. The path they had been walking, the man assured them, would bring them right to Gulls Landing.

Once out on the trail again, the girls faced Nolan and Gavin, who had nothing with them but the clothes on their backs.

"Okay, now tell us what you're doing here," Analyse said.

"Before you get mad, let me say something," Nolan began in halting sentences. Seeing the angry looks on the girls' faces, he was having trouble speaking freely.

Kate stood, arms folded. "What were you thinking? Did you think you were out for a stroll in the park or something?"

"We were at the Great Gorge," Nolan finally said.

Analyse interjected, "Which peewee here must have told you about since he was snooping in Kate's journal."

"That place stinks! There's some creepy stuff going on at the bottom of that Gorge," Nolan continued excitedly. "I took some pictures of it with my phone. They're building something huge, with hundreds of people."

The boys told what they'd seen, which is what the girls had already seen but only the beginnings of. They described a tower with stairs around it. Grod Vurmis was working fast. With the Dreglings under his control, he was probably building some kind of a fortress.

"The people were chanting some really dark stuff!" Nolan said. "Just freaky."

Gavin added, "And doing a weird dance. But we hid by the caves and they never saw us."

The boys went on to tell the girls how they'd gotten lost trying to leave the caves above the Great Gorge. They had to spend the last night with no blankets or food, huddled in the roots of a large tree.

"I tried calling," Nolan said, "but my phone wasn't working."

Analyse smirked at Kate.

Gavin explained how they met the old couple. "We used our brains and our feet," he said, repeating the formula their dad had taught them.

"Actually we sort of got lucky," Nolan clarified. The old man had found them right where they slept. "So we helped them load their carts with firewood, and they took us from up there to here."

Kate huffed with disgust and walked up to Gavin. She looked him in the eye. "So. You promised you wouldn't tell anyone, and already you've told Nolan."

"You said not to tell Mom or Dad, and I didn't! I told Nolan, that's it."

"I made him a deal," Nolan interrupted. "I said if he told me what you were up to, I'd give him my video game."

Kate faced her brother again. "You cheated and lied and you stalked us, so you remember what we said—you'll suffer the consequences."

"You can take my toys, but I'll still have Nolan's video game," Gavin sneered.

"You can't come with us," Analyse asserted. "You can stay here with these old folks and ask them to take you back to Shelby."

"We're going to see the King!" Gavin said.

"You're saying that because you know that's what we're doing," Analyse said.

"We're going with you, or we'll tell everybody!" Gavin shot back.

There was silence. Kate and Analyse stepped aside to confer with each other. They knew if they included the boys, they risked making mistakes that could ruin their journey. But Kate could never live with herself if her brother somehow got lost or disappeared because she had left him on his own. How would she explain that to her parents? And, if the boys did make it back to Shelby on their own, they would be sure to blab it to everyone and their quest was finished forever. They would have to take the boys but not before getting answers to a few more questions.

Analyse said, "So first, tell us why you came. Why did you follow us?"

Nolan glanced at Kate and looked away sheepishly.

Analyse said, "So I thought. We're not taking along boys who are chasing girls."

Kate had to call out Analyse. "Or girls who are suckers for handsome young men with berries," she said.

"Okay, I get it," said Nolan. "I agree."

Kate turned to the boys. "The most important thing is you have to be on board with our plan. Are you good with that?"

Nolan asked, "Why do you want to meet the king and queen? My dad says the royal family's just serving a life sentence in a gilded cage."

"We're on this trip to find answers," Analyse said.

"To what?"

"To everything. To what you saw in the Great Gorge, for example, and what the Kingdom of What Is . . . is."

Nolan and Gavin were not easily persuaded. They did not feel the same attraction to this land the girls felt. They had come because they were curious, for the adventure, nothing more.

Suddenly, they heard talking down the trail.

"The sea was just sparkling," a woman's voice was saying, then a man's voice, "And we had it almost all to ourselves."

They were three hikers with full packs.

"Hello," Kate said as they approached. But the three did not respond. One of the hikers was turning over seashells in his hands. The hikers did not see or hear them and passed right by.

"Hey!" hollered Nolan as the hikers continued on. He reached to stop one of them, but his hand went right through the person's arm. Nolan gasped and fell backward to the ground. "Ghosts!" he yelled, scrambling to his feet to run.

"Tourists," Kate said. "They can't hear you. They came to Time Out Woods but not into the Kingdom of What Is. So they can't see you, and they don't see anything we see."

"Here but not really here," Analyse added.

Nolan shook his head, panting for breath. "That's just too weird, dude, crazy. This place . . . it's just . . . "

Gavin said, "See, I told you, we had to go through those rose bushes. If we hadn't, we wouldn't see any of this, but you wouldn't believe me, so it's a good thing we did."

"The important thing is," Analyse said, trying to regain a sense of calm, "we all took a chance, right, and we're all here, right . . . together. We didn't plan it this way, which may not please everyone, least of all me. But let's just live with it and go. Gulls Landing can't be that far, and it's going to be dark in a couple hours."

Kate was proud of her friend's forthrightness and her acceptance of the situation. Kate suggested they get together and form a circle.

"Do we really have to do this?" Nolan asked.

Analyse instructed, "Just do it, okay."

They put their hands together in the middle of their circle. First, they all agreed that their goal was to try and find the palace and meet the royal family. Two, they promised their quest would remain top secret. If it got out that four school kids were running off to explore the woods during school hours, they all understood, this would end everything. Three, they agreed to stay together and look out for each other, no matter what.

"Agreed," Nolan and Gavin said. Nolan thought of giving their group a name, to which Kate agreed reluctantly.

Gavin offered several ideas like "Star Troopers" and "Avengers," but those names were vetoed.

Nolan suggested "The Voyagers," but Analyse pulled up her nose. "We're not on a cruise."

"How about the 'Four Fugitives' then?" Nolan said.

The others looked doubtful.

"It fits," he argued. "We escaped Brody's jail, right, and Gavin escaped Mrs. Leitenberg's grade five, so we're all on the run, right? Fugitives." He searched their faces for affirmation. "You know what Brody would say to us—'Okay people, you are out of bounds,'" Nolan said, mimicking their principal, sniffing as he spoke. "And it's true, dudes, we're *way* out of bounds here. We're fugitives. And it's awesome!" He threw his head back and yelped like a coyote.

The idea of fugitives on the run looking for a palace sounded a bit off. Kate imagined four fugitives finding a dark dungeon with chains waiting for them when they reached the palace. They voted, and the name "Four Fugitives" stuck by a vote of three to zero, with Analyse refusing to vote because she thought giving their group a name was too dorky.

"We go in the name of the King," Kate said.

They all echoed, "We go in the name of the King."

Chapter 12

To the Sea

They had walked for no more than an hour from the kind elderly couple's home, and Gavin was already slowing down. He and Nolan had not been thinking about a long journey when they entered Time Out Woods, so bringing some food was the furthest thing from their minds.

"I'm not going any further. I'm hungry, I'm telling you," Gavin complained.

"Come on, we're almost there," pleaded Analyse, not really sure she was right. "We'll get food when we get to Gulls Landing, all the food you can eat."

The four of them had finished the jerky and bread that Aster had packed for the girls, and all that was left were the roots. Analyse held one out to Gavin.

"Take a couple bites and chew on it as we go and swallow the juices. It'll pick you up."

"I'm not eating that stuff."

"Never mind," said Kate, pulling a granola bar from a pocket in her backpack and handing it to Gavin. "It's my emergency food."

"This isn't an emergency," Analyse protested. "It's being whiny, and if he wants to survive, he has to suck it up and eat what people here eat. Why didn't you eat more for lunch when you had the chance?"

As Gavin ate the granola bar through tears, three seagulls circled above them with loud cries. It sounded to Gavin like they were mocking him, and he threw a stone at them, yelling for them to go away.

"Quiet," Kate said, "they're trying to tell us something."

"This way! This way!" the gulls cried in unison and flew in the direction of a path the four of them had not noticed. It led left off the main trail down a slope and into the woods, which lay between them and the sea.

The gulls circled back. "This way! This way! To the sea . . . to the sea . . . "

"Look," Nolan said, "They're trying to show us which way to go."

"Taking a shortcut isn't staying the course," Kate objected.

"How do you know it's a shortcut?" Nolan asked. "Maybe it's actually the right way."

Gavin and Analyse agreed with Nolan, all eager to get to their destination. They wanted to follow the gulls.

"Maybe Grover just didn't know about this shortcut, so he didn't mention it," Analyse said. "And if Gavin's crying the whole way, I'm not walking any more than I have to. Remember, Aster said we had to fill in the details, and this kind of thing is a detail. What difference does it make if we go this way or that if it ends up at the same place?"

"If they end up at the same place," Kate repeated.

"They're *gulls*," Gavin said to his sister. "Don't you think they'd know where Gulls Landing is? Duh."

The gulls swooped in again. "On our way, to the sea! You'll see . . . you'll see . . . " Their cries faded in the distance over the woods.

Kate was outvoted, and they set out following the path the gulls had pointed them down. Even though the trail seemed to be as the gulls said—a direct route to the sea—the woods were thick and the way was steep and very rough. They had to concentrate as they scrambled over roots and rocks. At one point Nolan stumbled and fell forward but got back up quickly without a word.

They stopped under a large cedar tree whose boughs drooped above them like large hands. Nolan sat poking at the dirt with a stick, looking regretful of his choice to come on this adventure. Analyse would not look at the boys, and Kate was getting discouraged.

Nolan pulled his hand away from the stick he was holding and examined his palm. It had specks of a sticky black tar-like substance that stung. At the same moment, Kate felt a twig drop on her head. She picked it up for a closer look. At its broken end she noticed a dark-colored pitch. She put her finger to it and pulled her hand back immediately. It burned like hot cooking oil. She pushed her hand into the cool soil. She looked up. The trees were dripping the black pitch in several places where branches had broken off. She and Nolan jumped.

"Guys," Kate said, "it's the black guck."

Analyse screamed. "Kate, your hair!"

Kate's long brown hair had black streaks running down one side. She put her hand to it and her fingers stuck in her hair as if there were gum in it.

"Get out of here everybody!" Kate yelled.

They ran from under the tree. Nolan found a hole in his shirt where a drop of the black stuff had eaten through. He felt his shoulder burning and poured water from his bottle over it, which only made it burn worse. Kate pulled a small clump of hair away from her head. She sat on the ground and buried her face in her arms. They had walked right into a horrible place that the Plague had hit with an especially strong force.

"What is this stuff?" Nolan said, looking around.

Several trees were thin of branches, and the black poison oozed from wounds in their trunks. The woods were like a forest of melting candles, and the ground was a carpet of black splotched leaves.

"This is a horror movie," said Gavin. "I don't want to see any king or queen and their dumb palace." He got up without announcement and began walking back up the trail the way they'd come.

Kate went after him and turned him around.

"You aren't going anywhere, buddy. We agreed. We stick together, and we're all going that way." Kate pointed down the path through the woods to the sea.

Nolan got up. "Let's hurry up and get through these woods. I don't want to spend another minute here."

They carried on with Nolan now in the lead, then Kate, and Gavin tightly between Kate and Analyse so that he could not wander off. The trail switched back and forth along a quickly flowing stream. The Plague seemed to have affected the woods in patches. Those areas on higher ground were almost untouched, while trees nearer the stream suffered the most. Streaks of dark yellow moved with the flow of the water, like ribbons lacing through the current. Nearer the banks the water was a murky brown.

"This is how this forest got poisoned," Nolan said. "The trees are sucking up this putrid water from the stream and it's killing them."

"It starts white at the Gorge," Analyse said, "then goes yellow, then brown, and keeps turning darker and darker until it comes out black in the leaves and branches."

They watched for black pitch dripping from the overhanging limbs. In places it was like a slow rain, which forced them off the trail to avoid being pelted by it. They put on hats and caps for protection, but where their caps were hit, holes burned through.

The silence of death hung all around them, but there was nowhere to turn. They had to move on. Yet, in the middle of all this, there were signs of life. Kate heard birds and other animals she recognized and said their names aloud—thrush, woodpecker, wren, a coyote in the distance, a blue heron squawking as it took off into the dusk. In the gathering darkness, by calling their names, she held them close like familiar friends in a strange land, and felt consoled.

"That heron means we're close to water," Kate said with a brightness in her voice that surprised her. "And that means we must be near the sea."

They had passed into a small clearing and looked up when they heard a terrific whirring. It pulsed louder and softer, louder and softer.

"Cover your heads!" Kate yelled. Against the dusky sky they saw waves of bats, some flying within inches of them. Soon, hundreds had gathered, swirling in the clearing. Then, just as quickly as they had appeared, the whirring of wings died to a near stop. Hanging everywhere in the surrounding trees, the bats dangled like hundreds of socks on crisscrossing clotheslines. They chirped as one large chorus. Nolan shouted to try and scare them off.

Among the cacophony of chirping, they heard voices as clear as day: "Get! Get! Pushed out, pushed out. Get!"

"They're being pushed out," Kate said.

"Yick, yick," they heard. "Death by yick. Get." The bats chirped this desperate, mournful chant, which they continued as they fell helplessly to the ground. Slowly, one after the other, they tumbled from their perches, stone dead. Gavin picked up two of them and held them by their wings. The bats' stomachs had erupted from the inside with the black poison mixed with globs of partially decomposed insects.

"Wow," Gavin said, mystified.

Nolan took out his phone and took several photos of the bats hanging from Gavin's hands and of the hundreds dangling from the trees around them.

They walked on quickly. Kate paused to look back. Another cloud of the poor creatures were swirling desperately into the clearing, crying, "Get, get." The woods reeked of death.

Further down the trail, a friendly, rhythmic swoosh of waves sounded in the distance.

"We're close," Kate said. "Keep walking. I'll catch up."

She drank the last few drops from her water bottle, and as she turned to follow the others, she felt something watching. She looked to the side and saw two yellow eyes peering out from a small burrow in the rocks. Beneath the eyes, white teeth appeared in a wide grin as Kate heard a rumbling growl. It was a wild cat of some kind, most likely a cougar, Kate thought. She knew that a cat's grin can be a sign of hunger. The cougar's expression was not menacing but weak and desperate, as if all the health and comfort it had ever enjoyed had abandoned it. Kate was transfixed, their eyes locked. For a moment, she imagined she was looking at herself and wanted to comfort the beast.

It seemed to be saying, "Stay. You needn't worry, I'm in no position to chase you." Its ribs showed in ripples under its fur. It was starving. "I couldn't chase you even if I wanted to. I can only dream of . . . of the way things were."

The large cat faltered, panting heavily, and laid its head on the ground.

"Move on, dear one. Rain's coming, and the poison comes down heavy with the rain. Unless, of course, you would join me in the shelter of this cave . . . before I . . . "

Kate wanted to stay with the large cat in its last hours so that it wouldn't die alone. But she also knew this wasn't possible. She needed to be with the others. A tear ran down her cheek. As she turned down the trail, Kate heard a long, deep, and terrible groan, but she did not look back. She knew it was the cat's last breath.

She cried as she ran and ran. When she finally reached the others, she did not tell them about the cougar.

They soon heard the welcoming sound of waves hitting the shore as the trail opened out onto a sand covered beach. Before them was the expanse of ocean they had walked an entire day to find. The sky was dim and gray in the waning evening light. Rain was coming. Along with their relief at finding their destination came the dreadful smell of dead fish.

They heard Gavin yell, "Hey, look at this."

He had found a small overturned boat. Nearby were several others like it. They managed together to move a log to the front end of the boat and lift the bow onto the log. This formed a lean-to that they could easily crawl under. Getting wetter in a slow rain, they did the same with a second boat, and these became their shelters. Each overturned boat created more than enough cover and allowed the boys and girls to have separate quarters.

They had only two blankets, which the girls had taken from Grover and Aster, so the boys took one and the girls the other. Just as they got settled, the rain began coming down harder.

"Where are we?" Kate asked Analyse, huddled next to her beneath the canopy of their boat.

"I don't think we'll know until tomorrow."

They heard laughter coming from the next boat. Nolan yelled that Gavin had farted, and he wanted a different boat.

"You're on your own," Analyse shouted back.

Their tiredness and their relief at finding the sea overcame the chill of the night air and the cold of the sand beneath them. They fell asleep to the rhythmic swoosh of waves over the sand and the steady drumming of rain on the hull of the boat.

In the middle of the night, Analyse screamed and woke Kate with a start. The lapping of the waves had turned to a violent crashing. The rain had stopped, but the wind was howling, whipping sand beneath the gunnels of the boat and stinging their faces. As the wind continued relentlessly, it took on the personality of a bellowing, marauding tyrant. Kate peeked out. The waves were getting closer. The boys were standing outside, wondering which way to run. But just as quickly as the storm had started it died down again to a whisper. The clouds were blowing past like chariots in a sky-flung army on a scorched earth mission, leaving behind a still, star-studded sky. Suddenly, the wind died down and the waves were reduced to a gentle swooshing again.

"That was crazy!" Nolan said and howled like a coyote. "Look, the sky is so bright you can see everything."

To their left and right were the outlines of peninsulas jutting out into the sea, forming a horseshoe shaped bay, with them camped in its curve. The beach behind them rose sharply to grass-covered dunes with a path carved through it, which was the trail they'd come down. At the top of the dunes to their left a building like a small house lay silhouetted against the night sky. They would have to explore more in the morning.

They woke to light seeping under the boat gunnels and crawled out to fresh air. There were perhaps ten boats, like the ones they were using, dragged up onto the sand. There were also a couple of sail boats anchored off shore. There were no signs of life at the little house at the top of the dune. The stream they had followed emptied into the sea nearby. They were thirsty but also afraid they might pick up traces of the black poison if they tried to take water from the stream.

"Tell Gavin to get up," Kate told Nolan, who was propping himself against his boat, still rubbing the sleep from his eyes.

"He is up," Nolan mumbled. "He went walking."

Gavin was nowhere in sight. Kate started to panic just when they heard his voice from down the beach.

"Look, you guys, water!" He held up a water bottle. "I got it from that house. There's a faucet outside it."

Nolan ran to him and ripped the water bottle from his hand. He held it up and examined the water briefly before taking several long gulps.

Analyse looked around suspiciously. "This place is deserted, there are dead gulls and fish everywhere, and I wouldn't be drinking that."

Nolan took another drink. "Tastes clean," he said.

"There's a guy sleeping in a chair in that place up there," Gavin said.

"A guy! What else?" Kate said.

"Some stuff on his shelves. Food, I think."

They ran up the dune, slipping in the sand, and went to the building. They looked through a window. It looked like a supply shop with fishing gear. Some food sat on a couple of shelves, and on a rocking chair in one corner was a man fast asleep with his head back and his mouth open. Analyse knocked on the glass, but the man did not respond.

"The door's open!" Kate said. She pushed it in and paused a moment before asking, "Excuse me, do you have anything to eat here?"

The man did not stir.

"Mr., wake up, we're hungry, we need something to eat." She went to him and nudged his arm lightly. The man fell to one side, slumping over the arm of his chair. His nostrils and lips were black.

Kate screamed and ran out. "He's dead!"

Chapter 13

Gulls Landing

They ran from the shack, tripping down the sandy bluff to the beach, where they sat on a log shaking. Dying trees, dead bats, dead fish, and now a dead person. On top of that, they had no idea where they were. Waves washed onto the beach with a hypnotic whoosh, without a care of the sickness that seemed to be growing everywhere.

They were all tired from hardly sleeping, hungry from not eating, impatient and scared.

"What were we thinking taking that detour?" Analyse said. "That could have been the end of us, right there."

"If this is Gulls Landing, we're done anyway," Nolan said, "because everyone and everything's dead." He went quiet. He was beginning to feel an uneasiness in his stomach.

Gavin glared at Kate. "You said this would be an adventure! It's not an adventure, and we're going to die out here, and no one's ever going to find us!"

There was a sudden flash of white right beside them.

"Long time look, and long time no see. Yeesh, you are hard to find!"

"Corvus!" Kate screamed.

"I thought I'd find you on the way to Gulls Landing, not in this God-forsaken death trap. It took a small posse a few hours to find you," Corvus said while several other crows flew in and perched like sentries in the branches along the beach. "If this place isn't be the death of you, it appears you might be ready to kill each other anyway. All the squabbling—worse than a murder of crows."

Just then Nolan threw up into the sand.

"Hmmm, a touch of the Plague, I presume." Corvus squawked over his shoulder, and in a moment one of his pals flew in with a sprig in his beak, which he dropped in Nolan's lap.

"Chew on that right away and swallow it," Corvus directed. "You wait much longer, and it could go to your head. The herbs will take a few minutes to have an effect."

Nolan did as he was told but almost heaved again at the taste of the herbs.

"Just in case, here's a bit more," Corvus said, dropping a few sprigs of the medicinal plant into Kate's hand. "Remember to take it right away if you feel sick. It isn't much use once the Plague sets in. You'll know it's too late if you notice disoriented behavior, or if you find yourself craving more of the poison, oddly enough."

"Speaking of disorientated behavior," Analyse said, "What is this place?"

"Fisherman's Cove. The official word is, it's become so infected with the Plague that it's uninhabitable, out of bounds. I'd warn you not to drink the water, but I think you figured that out," he said, looking toward Nolan.

Nolan rested against a boat, still looking green around the gills.

"But the gulls, they pointed us this way," Kate said.

"Either they didn't know," said Corvus, "or it was a deception."

"So they're working for—"

"—for you-know-who. Not unheard of for Vurmis to turn animals to his cause."

"So where is Gulls Landing from here?"

"About a half-sun's voyage around Whale Back Rock." Corvus pointed a wing tip toward a high rock face along the north end of the cove. "Or much faster directly over the rock as the crow flies."

No one wanted to even think of hiking over or around a steep rock face after yesterday's dreadful walk through poisoned trees and bats. Another of Corvus's posse flew down beside them with a paper bag that she dropped at Kate's feet.

"We thought you might enjoy a taste of home," Corvus said. "Found it on a picnic table in the park . . . well, not exactly *found* it. I had to wait till the parents had turned around to look after their kids. Then I . . . dropped in and, well, picked it up from the table. It *is* called 'take out,' isn't it? There was some pretty ugly screaming from the mothers. They came after me, but my buddies put up some interference. Don't you have some story about a guy named Robin Hood?"

Kate peaked inside the bag. There was a box of chicken nuggets and some fries.

"Don't really care for those little snake things much," said Corvus. "Get stuck in my craw . . . but those little crusty critters, they're not bad."

Nolan was the first on his feet and grabbed the chicken nuggets. He ran off, with Gavin right on his heels reaching for the box. The box exploded in a brawl and the nuggets flew everywhere. The boys went scrambling after them, popping nuggets into their mouths as fast as they could find them. When the nuggets were gone, they ran back to locate the fries, but the fries were with the girls, who were under a boat wolfing them down.

"Well," commented Corvus, watching the melee, "I don't know which was better, stealing the food or watching this. Like a pack o' crows!" He cackled a long laugh.

The four sheepishly ignored each other. Nolan's stomach was not ready for fast food quickly eaten. He belched and vomited again, and the just-gobbled nuggets fell in a mess to the sand. No one said a word, and no one apologized, and rather than looking replenished and energized, they all looked disappointed and tired.

"Well, nothing like home cooking to cheer one up and bring people together," said Corvus sarcastically.

"We're all Vurmises, look at us," muttered Kate under her breath.

"It seems the four of you have some things to talk about," Corvus said, "so we will take our leave."

Kate did not feel like talking. She took out the map she had been making and spread it over the hull of an overturned boat. She had already drawn in the trail from Singing Meadow to the house of Grover and Aster. As closely as she could approximate, she drew in the path they'd taken on their regrettable detour, through the woods, and down to the sea. She drew in a stream and trees and labeled them "Dead Man's Creek" and "Batty Woods." She also wrote in "Fisherman's Cove," where they were at the moment.

"The boats!" Gavin said suddenly. "Let's take one of them. The owner is probably dead anyway, so we may as well take one."

They worked together to turn over a boat, then pulled and pushed it across the sand to the water. The tide was going out, so it would help draw them away from shore. But it meant they would have to leave soon before the tide turned back in. They threw their packs into the boat. Nolan slumped down on the back seat near the stern, chewing on a sprig of the medicinal herb, still a little green around the gills. All were aboard except for Analyse, who stood paralyzed on the beach.

"I can't swim," she said, shaking.

Just then they heard the mad cawing of Corvus and his company, who were flying toward them.

"Go quickly!" Corvus shouted as he flew past. "The enemy is at hand."

They could hear shouting from the woods along Dead Man's Creek, where they'd come down the day before. The voices were coming closer.

"Come on, Lyse! Now!" Kate said, "Grab my hand."

Analyse stalled, shaking her hands in the air, and with a shriek she finally climbed into the boat.

Only Kate and Gavin had any experience rowing a boat, so they took charge. The boat's oars were heavy, making it a struggle to get them into their locks, but finally Kate and Gavin were side by side, each on an oar, rowing hard. After a few awkward strokes and meandering turns, they got the boat pointed in the right direction and pushed out to sea. Analyse sat in the bow, clinging tightly to the sides.

They rowed toward the rocky point of land Corvus called Whale Back Rock at the north end of the horseshoe shaped cove. Around this point, Corvus had said, they would find Gulls Landing. They were well out from shore when they saw why the crows had warned them to go quickly. About twenty people were on the beach—Dreglings. Some were whole, and others were Shadows at different stages of vanishing.

The Dreglings were turning over boats, examining them, and taking what they could find, while others were looting the shack on the bluff. Two or three who were ordering the others appeared to be the leaders. One looked up and noticed the boat heading out and pointed. The others stopped and looked. Gavin and Kate pulled harder on the oars. They were rowing into a fog, which gradually shrouded them like a billowing blanket until they could see no further than a few feet in any direction.

To their good fortune, the fog hid them from the view of the Dreglings. But the fog also hid their view of Whale Back Rock, which they had to navigate around. They heard the voices again behind them and then the sound of oars getting closer. Somewhere beyond the fog they were being followed.

Suddenly, Analyse shouted from the bow. "Look out for the rocks!" They had drifted too close to the point, which suddenly loomed above them to their right. Ahead were two rocks a little larger than their boat that rose above the surface of the water, white surf whirling around them. Kate and Gavin tried to steer the boat away, but it was too late. The bow struck hard. Nolan was jolted off the back seat onto the floor of the boat, and Analyse went headlong over the side into the water. She came up gasping. Kate and Gavin grabbed her by the hand and finally helped her back into the boat, where she sat shaking, scared and cold.

Analyse screamed, "My glasses!"

"They're here," Kate said. Analyse's glasses hung by a tangled strand of her hair. The sight of Analyse, soaking wet with her glasses dangling, made Gavin laugh.

"Shut up, I could've drowned," Analyse said, shivering while she tried to adjust her glasses.

"We've got to get out of here, come on," Kate said as they rowed the boat away from the rocks with the surf splashing over the gunnels. Finally, they were out to the safety of calmer water again.

Through the fog, they heard the voices of the Dreglings following them. Kate and Gavin managed to make good progress with minimal noise, except for a faint squeak from one oar lock. A few minutes later they were around the point. Behind them, the voices of the Dreglings rose to shouts of confusion and chaos. They had apparently run into the same problem with the rocks near the point.

When the Four Fugitives were finally around Whale Back Rock, the fog began to clear, and they had caught a current that pushed them in the right direction. Gulls called sleepily overhead. Some of these same birds may have led them astray into Batty Woods, but at that moment gulls had never sounded so welcoming.

They could see the outline of the shore to their right. In the warmth of the sun Analyse dried out quickly, and Nolan was coming around. The herbs were having their desired effect. At this point they also realized how thirsty they were. They had not had any good water since taking the last swallows from their water bottles the day before. And they were hungry. The fries and chicken nuggets did not have lasting power. The girls took the roots from their bags and offered some to the boys. They chewed on these as they went, sucking the juices from the pulp.

Far off over land, they could make out a familiar cloud of smoke, marking the direction of the Great Gorge. Grod Vurmis was still gorging himself, his effects being felt not only in the Great Gorge but as far away as Fisherman's Cove.

After less than an hour they saw docks and buildings lining the shore, which they thought must be Gulls Landing. Homes rose up the side of a hill overlooking the sea. The village was much larger than they had expected. And they were supposed to find Grover's cousin Bowman in all of this?

Exhausted, they pulled into the harbour filled with all manner of sailing vessels, fishing boats, and a few canoe-like boats. The place was thriving with merchants, fishermen, and townsfolk all going about their business. The four newcomers were hardly noticed as they climbed out of their small boat, dwarfed by the surrounding vessels, and walked past fishermen and fishing nets on the dock. Figuring these folks would probably know the boat builders of the area, they enquired with someone sorting out his nets about Bowman.

"We go in the name of the King," Analyse added, remembering what to say.

"What would ye be wanting with Bowman? Looking to buy a boat, are we?" The man glared at them with a sun-scorched face.

Then they noticed the man was missing one ear and had a scar at the corner of his mouth that cast his face in a permanent scowl, as if he had been a fish himself at one time struggling on a fisherman's hook.

"Uhm . . . we're just looking," Analyse answered dumbly, as they moved on.

The man laughed loudly. "Hey Jib! These kids wanna buy yer shell of a boat," he snarled across the dock and jabbed at his nets like an angry shark.

Jib explained to the four, "Hal's too far gone to be of any use to you. Don't pay him any mind. Vurmis got to his mind. Got his hook in him once, and once it's in, it's hard to shake. Once a Dregling, it's just a slow fading to shadow."

"But how did he . . . ?" Nolan began.

"Used to be a really nice guy, gentle—a friend actually. Ain't that right, Hal? Am I your best friend?"

Hal simply snarled back.

"See, he hardly remembers who I am. He was sent back from the Gorge to catch other unaware takers, but he's pretty lousy at it, like he's become lousy at fishing. Now he just lurks in the shadows. Sad story, really sad. Used to be the best fisherman in Gulls Landing, and now I don't even recognize him from the man he was. His whole personality—changed, you know. I try to help him but . . . "

Jib's voice started to waver, and he pointed a thumb to a large building along the boardwalk. Sounds of woodworking and metal on metal echoed from inside. Two large wooden doors were swung open to the sea.

"You'll find Bowman there," Jib said.

Inside, a handful of workers were in the process of building two boats. A dog skipped toward them on three legs, and a man in a carpenter's apron followed. The four greeted the man they presumed to be Bowman with the royal greeting, and he returned it with sincere eyes as deep as two seas. He held out a large, rough hand to welcome them.

"Bowman, and this is Griff," he said, pointing to the dog.

Bowman had no forewarning of their visit, so the girls had to fill him in about meeting his cousin Grover and Aster and that they had been told how to find him. Before they'd finished their story, he'd given them as much water as they could drink.

"Come on, Griff." Bowman whistled to his dog. "I found him left for dead under the shop, one leg chewed off. Musta got in a tussle with a wild cat or something. So the boys and I, we adopted him, eh Griff?" Griff skipped ably along beside his master. Bowman led them up a small street behind the boat factory to his house and let them clean up. He set out some fried salmon and greens on four plates. They ate quickly, without any of the social graces their parents had tried to instill, and asked for seconds.

After the good food, they lay down exhausted, the girls on spare cots and the boys on mats on the floor, feeling safe and cared for. Griff lay between them, his head on his paws, ears twitching.

Grover was right. They were in good hands. Bowman had seen his task and risen to it immediately, seeming to know exactly what they needed. At the same time, Kate thought she noticed a current of sadness running through him, but his straightforward kindness and generosity betrayed whatever sadness may have lain inside him.

Chapter 14

Up the River Royal

It was still dark when they woke. They had slept from late afternoon to early morning. The smell of frying bacon permeated the house. Bowman whistled quietly, his large hands moving deftly about the kitchen as he prepared breakfast and packed some bags. His guests required safe passage up the River Royal—it was a mission he was taking to with gusto. They peppered Bowman with questions as they wolfed down breakfast.

"It's a slow death, that Fisherman's Cove," Bowman told them and shook his head. "Almost everything downstream all the way to the cove's been killed off. Hope you didn't drink the water."

Nolan raised his hand in mock confession, and Bowman chuckled.

"Good you got a taste of it so you know what's not good for you. If you all survived Fisherman's Cove, I think you can handle what's ahead. But you needn't worry about rowing a boat the rest of the way, we'll sail. Much less strain on the back." He whistled in disbelief at how they had made it this far. "That took guts, and some muscle."

Gavin pulled up his shirt sleeve and flexed his biceps. Then he removed his hat to show Bowman the effects of the black gunk. "It burned holes right through our hats."

Bowman nodded. "A cocktail of slag and other muck from the Gorge, from whatever he's building. But it's like he's mixed it with his own personal evil to increase the damage a hundredfold. See, once a place has the Plague and people find out, they don't dare go near it, and then Vurmis claims it. He's not dumb. His dad tried to take over by force, but Vurmis is more scheming. Eventually, he'll resettle Fisherman's Cove with Dreglings. That cove gives him a good launch point to invade other areas of the Kingdom.

Kate asked out of the blue, "Do you have a family?" After he took a breath and fidgeted with his plate, Bowman began talking freely about the thing he obviously loved most.

"I have one son, Adwen," he began with a smile. "He's in the service of Athar and Sapienta, as we all are of course, but I mean . . . he's in a particular service. Since Grover sent you and because you could be up for a similar task yourself, I can tell you a little more. But let's clean up here first."

After the table was cleared, Bowman sat down again with them, a cup of coffee in his hand.

"King Athar is gathering troops for a major assault against Vurmis," he confided. "It will be soon, your timing is good. The King commissioned the Prince to lead a special force with Adwen at his side. I assume that's why you're going to the palace," he said, studying their faces.

The four looked back and forth at each other. Kate wondered what use they could be, if any, in an assault against Vurmis.

"Forgive me, you're right, you should keep it under your hats. We don't want our secrets getting out to the enemy. The element of surprise is vital."

"Where's your wife?" Gavin suddenly asked. "Are you split up or what? Cuz my mom and dad, they're—" Gavin stopped as Kate poked him in the ribs.

Bowman smiled reassuringly. "My wife, Kyla . . . she fell into the hands of Dreglings." He took a sip of coffee, while the others stared in shock. "She was at the tailor getting a coat for our Adwen . . . he was ten years old at the time."

Gavin asked, "They took her away to the Great Gorge?"

"No, not exactly. She didn't have to be taken. She went with them," Bowman said. There was silence. "Kayla was always a trusting soul, you have to understand. She gave people the benefit of the doubt. But it's Vurmis's way—they see a weakness, and you're suddenly gone. My Kyla—she knew the tailor guy, a little too well I guess. He was attractive, had smooth hands, not like these." He held up his calloused hands. "The guy showed her a lot of kindness, fake kindness."

"Why did she fall for it?" Gavin asked, incredulous.

Analyse glared at Gavin and said, "You mean, fall for it like you never would have done?"

"I would not have! I would have kicked him where it counts!"

Analyse scoffed.

Bowman said, "By the time I found out what was going on, it was too late. She was gone. Maybe she wanted to go." He put his cup down, having said as much as he wanted to, and looked ready to leave. Griff prodded Bowman's leg with his nose.

"No, Griff, you'll be staying with the boys at the yard for this one," Bowman said as he patted the dog on the head and rose from the table.

At the docks, they loaded onto Bowman's sailboat, a 30-foot sloop with two sails, fore and aft. Gavin immediately jumped up onto the bowsprit, which projected forward like a powerful spear. Bowman warned him he wouldn't be sailing up there that way for long before he'd take a dive into the drink.

Their backpacks were freshly filled with supplies—dried fish, biscuits, and a kind of nut bar Bowman said would give them an instant lift when needed. Bowman also made sure the boys had blanket rolls, which were made of the same fine, dense wool the girls had from Grover and Aster. The girls showed him their roots. Bowman looked them over with interest.

"We don't have these around here. Keep them. They're very good for travel."

As they shoved off, Bowman addressed his youthful crew of four. "All hands! Everybody busy now!" Bowman gave them tasks simple enough for sailing novices, pointing to the gadgets and lines they were to haul on or untie. They were curious about everything on the boat.

"Only one rule!" Bowman announced. "No technical questions. We'll learn by doing, alright? Unlike my cousin Grover, I've never been much for books. I read the sails! Whenever the sails luff, it's like we're turning a page." As he said this and took a sharp turn out of the harbour, the sails rippled in the breeze before filling. "See that ripple? We just started another chapter, mates!"

He laughed a long guffaw to the sails. They felt an immediate surge as the wind caught them full sail. Bowman's hair swept sideways like a flag in the wind, and he sang loudly—

Way la hey, water ways!
Way la hey, gulls and terns!
Way la hey, whale and seals!
With us go, and guard our stern.
Way le hey, water ways!
Through the shoals and swells,
All in Athar's name we go.

Let west winds fill our sails.

They pushed away from Gulls Landing up the mouth of the River Royal, which was so wide at this point it was difficult to see to the other side. Kate imagined it must be like the Saint Lawrence River though she'd only ever seen the Saint Lawrence on a map. Many other boats filled the river. Bowman passed closely by one of them—a tall ship with majestic sails glistening in the morning sun. It flew a flag with the image of a rose. Bowman waved.

"Way hey!"

Several sailors looked down over the side of the ship and waved back.

"That one's from the royal fleet, see the flag?" Bowman said.

Nolan wanted to know why they didn't see any cannons. Bowman explained it was not equipped with canons but loaded with cargo—food, medicines, and doctors. The ship was headed for villages along the coast. "Those people have been having a rough time with Dreglings. If there's not some kind of royal intervention, those villages will end up like Fisherman's Cove."

"Why don't they get some canons and just blast them?" Gavin asked.

"I suspect the King and Queen have other plans," Bowman said.

"Like what?"

"You'll have to ask them. Like I said, secrets."

Bowman yelled for everyone to hang on as their bow went through a large swell that sent a spray of water over the boat and drenched them all. Bowman laughed at the expressions on the faces of his four passengers, gripping onto the boat in shock from the cold water.

"You've all just been baptized! No worries, you'll dry off. Just have your hand near a rail and hang on if we hit another one."

Bowman at the wheel was obviously in his element, reading the sails, jaw jutting forward confidently and happily. Kate smiled to herself and thought he must feel his loneliness was left on the dock when he was with his boat on the sea.

A warm wind came up. Nolan shouted, "Awesome, that will really dry us out," and held his shirt up, letting it flap like a flag.

Kate remembered the blast of warm air on their visit to the Great Gorge and looked ahead toward the mountains. The sky had a yellowish tinge where she thought the Great Gorge must be. Whatever plan the King has to stop Vurmis, Kate thought, it better happen soon.

"Kate, on the wheel." Bowman said. "All remaining hands, into the galley."

Kate took the wheel, shakily, as Bowman pointed ahead over her shoulder to a spot on the horizon. "See that tall tree right there along the river?" Kate nodded. "Keep a straight course for her. If you run into problems, holler."

He patted her shoulder, went below with the others, and laid out some lunch before taking out a large flask of water and pouring four cups. He told them they needed to drink up because they looked dry from the wind.

A few minutes later, Bowman stepped back up on deck to check on Kate. The boat was off course, and Kate hung slumped over the wheel. Bowman caught her just before she fell to the deck. He brought her below and laid her down on a bunk.

"What happened?" Analyse asked.

Bowman called for water. Kate drank groggily and slowly sat up. Bowman looked worried as he examined Kate's eyes.

"There's something toxic in the wind—more Plague," he said, taking a box of herbs similar to what Corvus had given Nolan. He crushed the herbs in a bowl and mixed them in water. He held the mixture under Kate's nose and told her to breathe in. She breathed, coughed twice, and Bowman held the bowl so she could drink the mixture. After a few minutes she started to look like herself again.

Bowman said, "You must have caught quite a lung-full."

After Kate ate something, she felt her strength returning and her dizziness going away.

The river was narrowing as they drew closer to the palace, but it was still quite wide as rivers go. Bowman shouted for everyone to hang on tight. A tall ship ten times their size was coming toward them dead on as if they didn't see them. Bowman quickly turned but not soon enough. The ship sideswiped them. Bowman's small boat tipped to one side. Gavin was holding to the rail while his feet dangled in the water. Analyse got caught in the foresail or she would have gone into the river. Nolan was stretched full across the top of the cabin, hanging for dear life to the mast. And Kate was knocked to the deck on the high side between the cabin and side of the boat. The boat righted itself again with Bowman at the wheel.

"Try it again, ya devils!" Bowman shouted as he reset his course up river. "I sail at the pleasure of the King!"

"Everyone alright?" Bowman asked his crew. One, two, three . . . Gavin was missing. Kate screamed. Behind them near the ship, a head bobbed up and down in the water and two little arms flailed where Gavin had dropped in. Alongside the tall ship, he looked like a water flea. Someone from the ship dangled a rope with a life ring.

"Don't take that, Gavin!" Bowman shouted.

He brought the boat sharply around with a skillful maneuver of the sails and wheel and steered in Gavin's direction. They were moving fast with the current. They would have just one chance to grab him, or they would have to come around for another pass, which might be too late.

"Kate, steer right up alongside him." She took the wheel as Bowman reached over the side of the boat. "Gavin, grab my hand, quick!" Gavin missed his hand, but Bowman managed to get a grip on the collar of his shirt. He held on to Gavin like holding a duffle bag, dragging him through the water for several feet before Bowman could hoist him aboard. Gavin sputtered and coughed in a panic.

Dreglings swore from the deck of the tall ship and threw down balls of flaming oil made from rags. One landed on the deck of their boat and sat blazing. Without a second thought, Nolan ran to it and kicked it like a football over the railing into the river, where it sizzled and died.

Bowman wheeled them around again, up river, until they were safely out of reach. Kate helped Gavin out of his wet clothes and wrapped him in a blanket.

Bowman explained the tall ship was one stolen from the royal fleet by Dreglings and, by sailing on a royal ship, the Dreglings could disguise themselves. People called them phantom ships because they seemed to come out of nowhere to harass and capture innocent victims. It was a close call for Bowman and his crew. He checked the boat for damage.

"We won't sink," he said, "but they scratched us up pretty bad."

Kate thought about Aster's prophesy and how one sibling fell from Aries into the sea and drowned. Not only her sibling but also her best friend had fallen into the water and survived. She hoped that that part of the prophesy had been fulfilled and done with because she didn't want to fear losing anyone. She asked Bowman about the prophesy.

"Yes, I know—the flying ram with the golden fleece," he said. "And Aries is definitely brighter than usual this year. Aster really pays attention to all that, and she's wise, I respect her. But sometimes the fate the stars signal can be overruled."

"Overruled!" said Gavin and pounded his fist on the deck like a judge bringing down his gavel.

"Yes, overruled this time, my friend," smiled Bowman. "And you live to tell it. Battles may be won or lost, but the war is ours. Never lose heart."

Nolan asked, "How did they steal that ship so easily straight from the royal fleet?"

"Spies, traitors. He may be evil, but Vurmis is also a strategist."

"Which of the royals is the boss anyway—the King or the Queen?" Nolan asked. "Like, who's in charge?"

"Ah, trick question," Bowman said. "It is rightly said, 'If you've met one, you've met the other—same in authority, of the same mind, though different in kind.' They think so similarly, sometimes you'd almost think you were talking to the same person. The ideal marriage, I guess you could say. And their boy's a chip off the old block."

"How old is the prince?" Analyse asked.

"No one knows for sure. Some say he's a boy, others say he's a grown man. I'd say he's ageless."

Ageless, like so many other things here, Kate thought. Oddly, it felt like she'd been here for ages herself even though it had been only two or three days.

"What year is this?" she asked.

"Another trick question? I like games," he smiled, confident of his answer. "It's the year of King Athar and Queen Sapienta, like always."

"So, when did they start being the King and Queen?" Kate pressed.

Bowman looked puzzled for a moment. "Think you can stump me, eh . . . hmm. No one really knows. They're . . . "

"Ageless?" Kate said, finishing his sentence.

"That's it!" He threw back his head and laughed. Bowman may have had sadness in his life, but he certainly knew how to love life. Kate could see the resemblance to his cousin Grover in the laugh, and they both had big hearts.

The sun was well on its downward arch behind them when Analyse yelled from the bow that she'd spotted something. She was pointing at several bumps going up and down in the river and moving along with the boat.

"Porpoises," Bowman said. "Our lucky day, we've got royal guides to the palace."

The pod grew larger, swimming on both sides of the boat. Bowman followed them as they guided the boat toward the north bank of the river.

The porpoises' sleek gray backs arched in and out the water as the pod began a low and steady "thrum, thrum, thrum" sound, both eerie and beautiful. Their combined movements and the thrumming itself seemed to create such a current that the boat was pulled along effortlessly.

Ahead, the river was bending sharply left. At the bend several docks appeared jutting out from the bank like fingers. Tied to the docks were several tall ships with workers busily loading supplies and preparing sails. Each ship flew the flag with the rose symbol.

Grover waved a hand and began singing a song, probably sung many times through the years by those who had come to this place.

> Ahead we go to his royal Grace.
> Lower the sails before his gates.
> Voices raise to King, Queen, and Son
> Where rest awaits at the setting sun.

As quickly as they had appeared, the porpoises disappeared, their work finished. On a bluff overlooking the docks was a long stone wall reflecting brilliantly in the late afternoon sun. Fruit trees huddled at its base, and rose vines covered the wall with a spray of bright red blossoms.

Chapter 15

A Royal Greeting

They tied up the boat at the docks among the tall ships of the royal fleet. After regaining their land legs, Bowman led them on a cobblestone road that wound up the bluff to where the palace stood. People were coming and going on the road. Watchmen stood in broken down towers at several places on the wall. Ruined or not, each tower had a flag with a red rose on a white background that waved in a steady wind. Nolan took out his phone to photograph the castle.

Kate put her hand over his lens. "What are you doing?" she said.

"Stop, I'm documenting this." He took several more shots of the wall and of the ships at the docks, and last he turned the camera on the two of them for a selfie.

"No one will ever believe it otherwise," he said. "This is our evidence." He gave Kate a hug.

"Hey," she said. "I thought we agreed . . . "

"It's just a thank-you hug," he said. "I'm sorry I didn't have more faith in you, but look, we made it! Now we're actually here, man, it's awesome! And I can't wait to see inside."

As they walked up the road, they held hands but dropped them when Analyse turned to see what was keeping them.

The site of the castle was well-chosen. It sat on a rocky bluff in the crook of an elbow where the river bent north and where a second river, the Downfield, joined the Royal on the far side. The bluff offered a clear view for miles up and down both rivers and eastward to the mountains.

The road rounded a corner in the castle wall. From this angle Kate recognized what she had seen on her first visit on the backs of the geese. The wall was badly damaged. In some places they could see daylight through holes to the other side of the wall, and it seemed no one had bothered to repair them. Bright red roses stood out sharply against the wall's shabbiness.

Kate felt a pit in her stomach. The castle didn't look any better from the ground than from the air, which made her feel guilty about dragging her friends with her all this way. She was hoping that maybe what she saw on her first trip was not the real palace. She had kept her first visit a secret because she did not want to discourage Analyse from coming. But she couldn't tell them now that she knew all along the palace was actually just a dump. What would they think of her? They would disown her.

"Is this the palace?" Analyse asked in disbelief.

"Yes," said Bowman with great reverence. "It is indeed."

From across the river, from the direction of the mountains, came a strong gust of wind. The wind was so hot it made them shrink down and cover their heads. The roses on the castle wall wilted before their eyes. Bowman shook his fist toward the mountains and let out a long deep throated howl, so intense that it scared the others. An elderly woman pulled her shawl over her head against the wind and yelled also, "Curse you, Grod Vurmis!" and carried on down the road.

When they finally reached the castle gate, people were passing in and out. A cart of produce was being drawn inside. The gate was merely a wide hole in the wall with no doors.

Bowman hollered up to a sentinel on the wall and waved. "We come in the name of the King!" The sentinel waved back.

They followed Bowman inside. The castle interior was much larger than was apparent from the outside. It was like an immense park with lots of trees. There were people of all types. There were young and old, men and women, well-dressed and poor, some busy in manual labor, some playing music, and others simply relaxing in the shade.

Bowman greeted a couple of people he knew. Gavin, who was trying hard not to stare, caught the eye of a young boy with a ball who approached him.

"We . . . we come in the name of the King," he said to the boy.

"I don't think you have to say that once we're inside," Analyse whispered.

The young boy kicked the ball Gavin's way, Gavin kicked it back, and he was instantly part of a group of screaming soccer players.

Kate, Analyse, and Nolan followed Bowman to the center of the palace grounds. They stopped at a large cobblestone courtyard nearly a city block in size. In the middle of the courtyard was a pool, and at the far side stood the actual palace, terracotta red in color, topped with a flag bearing the red rose emblem. The palace wasn't covered with gold and silver as in story books. Rather, it was adorned with carvings and carefully crafted frescos of colored stones from various parts of the Kingdom, grand and beautiful in its simplicity.

From the central part of the palace, two wings extended in opposite directions like long arms open wide. Each wing had two levels. In complete contrast to the castle walls, the palace itself looked intact and well cared for. Bowman said there was nothing like it anywhere, "like a beacon of hope."

The palace immediately replaced Kate's fears and regrets. When they drew closer, they noticed the carvings and frescos were actually stories in pictures, which Bowman said represented the most important events in the life of the Kingdom.

On both wing extensions, several doors swung out onto verandas. On these verandas they saw people convalescing in various stages of illness or injury.

"Is this a kind of hospital?" Kate asked.

"You could say so," Bowman said, "Some people come to get well. I stayed here for awhile once, and I'll never regret it."

There was a scream from a second floor veranda. Two men were trying to hold onto another man writhing in pain. They watched, terrified.

"Look, they've caught a Shadow!" Nolan said.

"Not caught," Bowman laughed. "He's been rescued or escaped. And now the man is recovering. It's not true what a lot of people say—'once a Dregling always a Dregling.' Not all Dreglings want to get well, of course, but for those that do, like the ones here, there's hope."

Kate wondered if he was thinking about his wife, Kayla, when he mentioned hope. Then she said to others that she wanted to meet a Shadow.

"Why?" Nolan asked.

"I don't know why," Kate said. "I just want to."

Sitting in the courtyard was a group of women. One wore bandages around her head. There was an eruption of laughter from the circle. One of them jumped up when she saw Bowman, ran over, and embraced him as though he'd just returned from a long voyage. She had black hair to her shoulders and was dressed in a finely embroidered dress.

She welcomed Bowman and the young travelers and invited them to have something to eat.

Kate quickly fetched Gavin from the soccer game, and they were showed into a large dining hall. Elaborately crafted tapestries hung from the rafters everywhere, each unique with its own image celebrating significant moments at the palace over the years. Kate and Analyse slowly turned a complete circle to take them all in. In a loft above the eating area, a quartet of strings was playing a lively classical piece. It resonated beautifully through the hall.

"This beats the school lunch room," Analyse said.

People sat at several tables. Beneath the tables were boxes with holes in their tops. They were meant as foot muffs, lined on the inside with fur. People would take off their shoes before sitting and slip their feet into these boxes as they ate. The weary travelers thought this was the most awesome feature of a dining table anyone had ever thought of. Bowman's friend, the woman who had invited them in, sat with them as they ate, listened to the stories of their journey, and called for the attendants to refill their plates.

"You are young but brave," the woman said. "Be sure to share your stories with the others. You can stay as long as you like."

"Is it possible to . . . " Kate began, "to meet some of the sick people here?"

"Certainly," the woman said. "Tomorrow I'll take you to meet someone."

Kate blushed at the woman's eagerness to accommodate her. After they'd eaten all they could, someone brought out "royal trifle," a creamy vanilla dessert with plums and cake that resembled English trifle.

"Nectar of heaven!" Analyse yelled spontaneously as she took her first bite, causing people from other tables to look up suddenly. They raised their spoons and shouted their agreement, showing mouthfuls of mashed up cake and pudding.

This was the most relaxed and happy they'd felt on their entire trip. The woman excused herself to attend to someone in the palace's "wings of grief," the name she gave for the two long extensions of the palace. A man, sweaty and covered in wood dust, approached as the kind woman was leaving. He gave her a gentle, warm embrace and kissed her on the lips before she carried on, now speckled with the man's woodchips. He greeted Bowman with an enthusiastic hug, and Bowman began to weep.

"It's good, Bo. Love conquers. It's all good now," said the man and held him tightly. They had a deep history together, it was clear. The man then turned to the four young guests, who were finishing their desserts, and greeted them with a wide, affirming smile.

"This is King Athar," Bowman said.

The four almost choked on their trifle. They were not prepared for the person they met. He was just an average guy—dark hair and medium build in ordinary working clothes. The only things special about him were his soothing voice and his deep brown eyes, which danced as he spoke to them.

"We are glad you came," he said sincerely, sounding as though he had been expecting them.

"So . . . " Analyse said, "that woman, that was . . . "

"Queen Sapienta, yes," Athar said. "Why don't we go out and sit in the courtyard, where we can enjoy the last bit of daylight."

Outside, Bowman left them so they could talk with King Athar by the pool, which had a spring of fresh water gurgling up from its center. The King cleared the surface of the water with his hand, took up a couple handfuls, and drank until water dripped down his chin. With four cups, he scooped up water and put them in the hands of his four guests.

"Do you know why you are here?" the King asked as though he knew the answer himself.

They felt stymied by the question, but finally Kate answered, "Actually, we don't know why we came, not exactly anyway, but Budsley . . . I mean . . . "

"Excellent," the King said. "Sometimes not knowing exactly why is the best way to come. Maybe you'll find the answer while you're here. You came—that's the important thing." If King Athar actually knew why they were there, it was apparent he was going to let them find out for themselves.

"We want to be in the special forces," Gavin said suddenly.

"And you very well may be," said the King. "Thank you for your courage and willingness."

The King and Queen were so down to earth and approachable, so common, that the Four Fugitives felt completely safe and at rest. They had expected a king and queen with royal garb and scepters, sitting on ornate thrones in a large elaborate court with uniformed attendants, but the royalty they found was so much better.

"Don't you have other people who chop the wood and serve lunch?" Nolan asked.

"Most certainly, many others," said Athar. "We all work together. We'll give you a try at wood chopping tomorrow if you like."

Analyse asked, "So, you don't have crown jewels or . . . anything like that?"

"Oh yes. We do have crown jewels, many."

Their faces widened.

King Athar extended an arm in a wide arch to the people on the palace grounds. "These are the crown jewels," he said with great pride. "You are too, and knowing you is my greatest pleasure." They could tell this was more than just a nice thing he said, and they were overcome with a sense of importance and pride. It was like he meant it for each one of them.

Athar asked a man named Horace to lead the four to their sleeping quarters. The tall, barrel-chested Horace took up the backpacks from the travelers and led them through a small grove of fruit trees. Through the grove ran a small, clear stream that came from the pool in the courtyard.

"Help yourself to water any time," said Horace. "It's the most delicious you'll find anywhere."

Their sleeping quarters were in a cabin-like building with a middle sitting area and a large fireplace. Off this central space were private rooms, one for each of them. Kate's bed was so soft and comfortable that she sank in and fell into a sound sleep immediately. She dreamt of being at her grandmother's house, where she had not been since her grandmother had died three years ago. Her grandmother had always spoiled her with Kate's favorite foods and large fluffy pillows. She had let her roam all day and let her stay up as long as she wanted.

It was morning when Kate heard a knock and the rumble of Horace's voice outside her door.

"Breakfast, madam. This time, special service. Next time, to the dining hall ye go."

Kate opened her door. Sitting on a stool was a tray with a scone topped with crushed plums and a cup of sweet milk similar to what they'd had at Grover and Aster's house. The other three found the same tray at their doors. They ate outside on the cabin steps. Their breakfast made fighting over nuggets and fries the day before seem ridiculous.

The palace grounds were already bustling with people walking, working, and relaxing on the verandas along the wings of grief. Though Shadows were common on the palace grounds, they attracted no gawking or comments of any kind from the others. The Shadows were residents like everyone else.

Finished with breakfast, Nolan belched loudly. Gavin tried his best to outdo him, and a moment later Analyse surprised them all with a long resonant belch that far surpassed both Nolan's and Gavin's. It echoed across the palace grounds all the way to the palace itself and caused a couple of people to look up from the healing wings and wave their approval. A voice shouted from the courtyard, "Winner!" The four laughed until their breakfast nearly came up.

Kate felt a freedom and contentment she had not felt for many months, perhaps had never felt before. She thought that if her mom and dad could only be here to experience this, it would be enough to bring them back together.

Chapter 16

A Crackling Sound

M ost of that day they spent relaxing under a broad oak tree just outside the King and Queen's quarters. Sapienta brought them several carefully selected books from the Royal Library. They immersed themselves in famous stories of the Kingdom—about the Rebellion and life before the Rebellion. There were also some stories about the perilous adventures of heroes and heroines. Gavin thought reading was too much like school and ran off to play with other kids.

They had as many cold drinks and snacks as they wanted. At one point, Sapienta asked them for their thoughts about what they were reading, and they answered with questions of their own.

"Are the holes in the castle wall from the battle with Grod Forza?" Nolan asked.

"Yes," said the Queen. "He attempted a siege of the castle in his day but failed. Many died. He was after the Royal Library, but he would have never found it. Would you like to see it?"

Queen Sapienta led them inside. She flipped a hidden latch on the wall beside a large fireplace and pushed. A panel of the wall pivoted to expose a passage leading down a narrow flight of stairs. At the bottom of these stairs was an underground library that made Grover's look like a little playroom.

Kate stood speechless at the endless rows of books. Not even the library at her dad's university was this large.

"This is what Grod Forza was after. He was coming after books with canons," Sapienta laughed.

"And what would he have done with the books if he got them?" Nolan asked.

"Burn them," said Sapienta, "out of spite. He resented everything the Kingdom stood for. He was simply hateful, and that's what drove him—that and greed. And of course, a lust for power—that's one thing both he and Vurmis have in common."

"We met a man . . . Grover," Analyse began.

"Grover! One of my favorite storytellers," Sapienta said. "Then he must have told you how Vurmis has picked up where his father left off. He's been stealing the Kingdom books, but instead of destroying them he's studying them."

"Studying them?" asked Kate.

"He's twisting the stories and trying to rewrite them with himself as the hero. I say *trying to*, mind you. A keen eye can always distinguish true stories from the counterfeits. The false ones just stick in your stomach like too much cake. But a keen eye like Grover's develops over years of faithful reading of the real stories, and he catches all the fakes."

"Is Vurmis coming again like his dad, to try and take over the palace?" Nolan asked.

"I suppose he'll try. But he's more patient and craftier than his father. Forza killed many, many in the Kingdom. But as we say, Vurmis has found greed and deception to be far more effective weapons than the guns and canons his father used."

They returned outside to the veranda, where a gust of warm air greeted them as they emerged, reminding Kate of the blast of hot air on the boat that almost knocked her out.

"It's strange," Kate said. "The days are short like fall, but it's hot like summer."

"Yeah, it's great," Nolan added. "It's like summer forever."

"Beautiful on the surface," Sapienta said, "but not underneath it all. This is not right . . . not good at all. The crisp chills of autumn must come so the land can rest. The leaves must fall and die and replenish the ground. Things must sleep and wake again with new life—forest flowers, fiddle heads, and fawn." She gazed into the sky, speaking with a lilt and rhythm as if quoting a poem. "The geese must fly south and return again. But instead the birds stay, thriving like never before, feeding on a harvest that never ends. I fear for them. The land cannot hold. A great calamity of starvation threatens. Everything must rest, rest. The close of harvest songs await and must be sung."

Sapienta seemed caught in a vision. She carried on, murmuring as if in a desperate prayer, then stopped and took a deep breath.

"Vurmis has fooled many into thinking these long summers are a wonderful thing, but this is all a consequence of his greed. When Vurmis is dispelled, all will be put right."

She took a moment to examine the three pilgrims before asking in a gentle voice, "What is the greatest sorrow of your hearts?"

They sat in silence at first. Then Kate and Analyse told her all about their parents. The Queen listened patiently before turning to Nolan, who went red. He did not want to say what his greatest sorrow was, but Kate could guess what he was thinking—that Kate did not like him as much as he liked her.

"You will all find love," Sapienta said finally with an assuredness that would have made Vurmis himself shudder. "A heart bereft of love is the greatest sorrow of all, but you *will* find love."

Sapienta swayed in her chair singing a mournful song in the traditional tongue. It seemed to speak of loneliness, filled with the many years of her people's suffering. At last she went quiet. She said, "Kate, I think it's time for you to meet someone."

Sapienta brought her to the second floor of the wings of grief. Kate had to cover her nose at the stench that permeated the halls. They stopped at the door of one room where the smell was especially strong. A woman was sitting alone facing the window. The Queen introduced her as Mirabelle. The woman adjusted herself in her chair, looked up at Kate, and said hello.

Kate swallowed, trying hard not to show her alarm. Mirabelle's voice was young and suggested a smile though Kate could not tell for sure if she smiled because her mouth was not there. In fact, except for deep brown eyes and dark hair, the woman was only a vague outline of her former self. What Kate saw in the chair was no more than a long sleeveless dress. Where her arms should have been, Kate could see through to the spindles of her chair. There were a few patches of skin on her forehead and elbows, but only her hair told Kate there was a person there, and the woman's eyes, which were gleaming lights that looked out in hope amid terrible sorrow.

"Thank you," Mirabelle said next.

"Thank you," Kate said back without thinking.

Mirabelle started telling her story, unhindered and sincerely, as though she had been waiting for Kate, as a trusted friend, for some time.

Mirabelle said, when it all started, she was fifteen and had been serving as a courier, running through lavender fields and over rough terrain to bring news between villages. She had always loved running. One year, her village was suffering from crop failure because of the Plague, and she was carrying a message to a neighboring village requesting food. She met two women on the way. They told her they could help because their own village, very nearby, had an abundance of food that year. They led her down a road to their home, and then it was too late. She had walked right into a Dregling village.

She was kept in a nice home, better than any she'd ever lived in, but someone was constantly watching her. They fed her with their best food and brainwashed her with stories of a new and different kingdom. They spoke to her of the families in their village who never had to suffer any more. They promised, if she stayed and worked a few more days, they would give her a horse so she would never have to run over the hills again, and she could go home after that if she wanted.

Mirabelle could just imagine what having a horse would do for her family, so she stayed and worked and worked. What she didn't realize was that, as days passed into weeks, she slowly forgot about home. She was thinking only about what the Dreglings and Grod Vurmis wanted people to think about— the new kingdom of Vurmis. Eventually, her body began to disappear. Also, she did not notice she was slowly losing her personality and her own will. Finally, she had completely forgotten who she was and how long she had been away from home, if she had ever actually left home. She had become one of the "disappeared." As far as anyone was concerned, she did not exist.

One day, while she was working in a potato field, a large swarm of but-terflies appeared, covering the field from one end to the other, something Mirabelle had not witnessed since she was a small girl. The sight ignited a spark in her, a memory of her past. A small remnant of beauty, like a seed, sprouted somewhere inside her. She began to long for the little girl she used to be—free and in love with the world and with her home.

She followed the swarm of butterflies, wandering farther and farther from the Dregling village, until hours later she came to a field of lavender. She recognized it, startled as if waking from a long dream, fully aware of where she was. It was her dad's field.

She hungered for just one bite of her mom's fresh-baked bread but hid outside her house for hours, watching her parents come and go. She was afraid they would not take her back if they saw her the way she was— a Shadow. But they looked so trodden down with sadness that her heart finally broke and she yelled out to them. They knew her voice immediately.

When they saw her in her disappeared state, they knew what had happened. They had been waiting for her for weeks.

Eventually, she and her parents took the long trip to the palace. Now she was hoping for the day when she would be whole so that she could go home again.

As Mirabelle told her story, Kate saw something that would have made anyone scream if she had not been so taken in by Mirabelle's story. With each part of her story, Mirabelle was recovering pieces of herself. The areas of her face began to return to what they once were. Her body made soft crackling sounds as small patches of skin appeared here and there on her arms. These fragments joined to form whole arms, and finally slender fingers appeared. Her skin was like a collage whose edges were slowly melding. Mirabelle groaned in pain as the crackling grew more intense and she continued to regain more and more of her body.

The curtains fluttered. A fresh breeze rushed in through the window, dispelling the acrid smell. In its place, wonderful aromas of lavender and fresh-baked bread filled the room—the smells Mirabelle had known so well since she was a child!

Mirabelle held up her hands and gazed at them recovering their true form. She pulled up her dress to her knees. Her legs and feet, though patchy, were whole and strong again like those of a runner. She wept—a spigot opened that would not shut off. She put her rough, reformed hands into Kate's, tears running down the thin cracks in her face like rivulets. As Mirabelle's hands shook, Kate could feel her nails growing back.

A memory came to Kate—she was with her dad, watching the salmon in Time Out Woods. The skin of the fish was shredded in patches as they struggled upstream to give up their bodies so their new young could live.

Sapienta said to Kate, "There's a story of tears in every room here. As they remember their stories, they remember themselves piece by piece. But their stories have power only because someone is listening, and you were here for Mirabelle."

As Mirabelle said good-bye with a broad, broken smile, any fear Kate may have had of Shadows was gone, for here she had made a friend of one. And though Kate had shared nothing about herself, mysteriously she felt as though Mirabelle had been listening and knew her story as well.

Stepping outside on her way out to the courtyard, Kate felt weightless, like she could fly, without the help of geese. She felt more herself than she'd ever known herself to be. She wanted to tell someone about what had just happened in the wings of grief, but she didn't know how to explain it.

She saw Bowman at the pool. He was pouring water over his head. He motioned for her to follow him.

"An important meeting," he said, "this way."

Along the wall near the gate, Nolan, Analyse, and Gavin were loading broken stones from the castle wall onto a cart. With rubble strewn everywhere, the job looked endless. A couple of stone masons worked beside them, replacing some of the stones into gaps in the wall. Kate grinned as she realized repairs were going on everywhere, inside and outside.

King Athar approached and asked them all to take a break. They made seats of the rubble and Bowman stood as the King spoke. Athar wiped his hands on his knees. He had some news.

"This is not the end of your journey," he said. "Prince Servan is returning to the palace tomorrow and will be gathering his special forces. I want you to be part of it."

Gavin leaped to his feet and let out a whoop. "Special forces!"

Nolan smiled and gave him a high five.

"Bowman will be commanding a fleet of ships to towns along the coast," Athar said, "where people have been needing help. Vurmis has had his way for far too long. Gavin, Kate, Analyse, and Nolan—you will be going with the Prince and other troops to the Great Gorge."

They sat gaping—to the Great Gorge? Analyse and Kate held each other's hand.

"I understand you probably want to know when, and how, and why. But you will not know the details in advance. The mission is top secret, even to the troops. You need only stay with Prince Servan and all will be made plain in due time."

Kate stared at the ceiling from her bed that night waiting for sleep. Their sublime comfort in this wonderful palace, so vibrant with life and love, was coming to an end. They would be going back out into the dangerous unknown, right into the enemy's stronghold, with no details and no notion of how to contend with such an enemy. The wind picked up and it rained hard most of the night. Kate wanted to yell through the downpour, "Dad, help me! I can't do this!" but her tongue would not move to form the first word.

Chapter 17

On a Mission

By morning, after a sleepless night, the rain had stopped. Puddles dotted the palace grounds, and the summer-like heat had returned in full force. Kate and Analyse had no sooner emerged from their sleeping quarters when they heard shouting from the tower watchmen. The Prince was arriving. The people on the grounds cheered and instantly began an enthusiastic chant in the traditional language. Bells tolled continuously from the towers. From the sky came a familiar song as a flock of geese flew over.

> Come in, come in to the royal courts,
> riding, walking, day and night.
> Strangers and kin, strong and fallen,
> draw near the halls of burden and light.

The musicians attempted to join in with their instruments, which had gone out of tune overnight. And the people tried to join in singing, but their voices were somewhat croaky so early in the day. In spite of their enthusiasm, the combination of geese, instruments, and human vocals was abysmal and made such a horrific sound that Kate and Analyse had to cover their ears. The King finally stepped in and told everyone to stop and let the geese carry the tune without the help of instruments or voices out of respect for the auspicious occasion.

Workers, caregivers, musicians, and Shadows—all gathered as Prince Servan and his troops appeared at the gates on eight horses. Three of the horses were being ridden double with extra passengers—Shadows.

"Where is he?" said Gavin, looking among the riders for Servan.

Athar and Sapienta walked forward and stopped to pat one horse in particular on the neck. The horse was a grey dun with a black mane and black around its eyes and nose, which gave the appearance of a horse that had seen many battles and hardships. Its rider removed a rain cape and dropped down to the ground, almost falling with exhaustion. The King and Queen held him in a long embrace, and everyone cheered.

Arm in arm with his father and mother, Prince Servan strode toward the spring in the courtyard. The other riders followed, dunked their heads in the pool, took long draughts of water, and sank down on the spot to rest or sleep. Among the Prince's company, Kate noticed one of the riders was taking some extra time to talk with Bowman.

The two approached Kate with proud smiles. "My son, Adwen," Bowman said. "I've told him to take care of you and your friends on your mission. He's become very close to the Prince, so he knows Servan's mind and heart like a brother, and he's never left his side. You can trust him for whatever you need. I must be off now," he added. "I have a fleet to ready for sail."

Before Kate could say good-bye and thank him, Bowman had turned and was off through the castle gate with resolve in his stride.

Athar led Servan toward the four newest and youngest arrivals to the palace. The Prince was soaked, dirty, and unkempt. He wore the same simple clothes as his troops did, and like the King and Queen he did not wear a crown. Aside from his striking resemblance to his parents, one would never guess this young man was the Prince.

He walked slowly and had deep furrows in his face. People were right about how difficult it was to judge his age. He could have been in his teens or in his thirties or even much older. He seemed as old as Kate's father by his appearance, but his voice was that of a young man. He came closer and greeted the Four Fugitives. His eyes and smile were youthful but were those of someone with much life experience.

"The entire Kingdom thanks you for your long journey," he said. Again, it seemed as though he too was expecting them.

"Have you been waiting for us?" Kate asked.

"Waiting, oh no, we don't know 'waiting' here," he said. "There is only 'the right time.' You came at the right time." Then the Prince surprised them by kneeling to the ground and putting his hands over their feet. He spoke softly something like a prayer. He looked up. "These feet honor us. I am at your service."

The four checked each other.

"At *your* service, sir," answered Kate and unconsciously curtsied, giving a respectful bow of her head, not sure if this was the proper behavior.

Servan noticed her discomfort. To lighten the air, he returned the same curtsy and bow of his head. Everyone around laughed and applauded gleefully.

The Prince and his small company had been riding most of the night through the rain under cover of darkness to avoid Dreglings. The Shadows they picked up had defected from Vurmis and had begged to be rescued. Servan and his troops would stay one more day and two nights at the palace to rest and resupply before starting on their mission.

During their stay at the palace, the four young pilgrims learned several things about Prince Servan from their reading and from others who knew his story. As a boy, the Prince could not get enough of the books from the Royal Library. He studied them constantly. But his parents impressed on him the need to do more than just study. He needed to know the land and its people up close. Reading the stories, they told him, was very important, but books were no substitute for actually living with the Kingdom's people.

So, with the Kingdom stories in his heart, the young Servan left the palace and went to live in a small village with a family willing to take in an extra person. He took a new name, Booker, for his love of books, to avoid gossip and unusual attention. He went to school and worked like all the other kids. While he was there, some thought they recognized him as the King and Queen's son, but few believed he was really the Prince because of how he blended in so naturally. He was a normal part of the community. And if he were the Prince, they thought, he would surely not have left the palace to live with common people.

When he was older, Servan traveled everywhere he could for several years and became deeply acquainted with the land and the people. He even spent a few days in the caves on the rim of the Great Gorge, perhaps slept in the very cave Kate and Analyse had stayed in! He spent much of his time with Dreglings. Some came to love him and reject Vurmis. But few believed Servan was actually the Royals' son until one day when Athar and Sapienta arrived at Servan's village for a special festival. Some observed that the King and Queen seemed to treat the boy like their own son. From then on, Booker's true identity as the Prince was rumored and debated throughout the Kingdom in homes and marketplaces.

The day had come to leave the palace. The morning was bright and unusually hot. Supplies were being gathered and arrangements made when there was a loud call.

The troops assembled, carrying only small backpacks. Kate, Analyse, Nolan and Gavin were the youngest among them, numbering twenty-five in all. No one wore a uniform of any kind. The only thing that marked them as special forces was a royal flag tied to each of two carts carrying their supplies.

Analyse whispered to Kate, "Does this look like an army to you? It's so bizarre. None of these people look like they've fought a day in their lives. We don't even know what we're supposed to do. Look at us—we're not ready for a fight. Kate, let's think about this, we're going to the Great Gorge!"

Kate said, "Look at me. I'm shaking, but I'm okay. Nolan and Gavin are in, look. We all stick together, right? And the King hand-picked us."

"Yeah, to die?"

"He wouldn't send us out just to die. He knows something we don't. We're probably meeting up with a real army, and we're the support troops or something. Come on, you can't poop out now."

Analyse was not easily convinced until horses were drawn from the stables. She loved horses and hoped this meant she would be riding. The two carts with supplies were hitched to two of the bigger steeds. The others were assigned one rider each. The horses stood strong and steady, as though they knew the mission they were on was one of royal magnitude. It was obvious by their composure these horses had received rigorous training.

Analyse was given a tan with a creamy mane. Kate's horse was brown with a black mane. Its coat rippled at her touch. Nolan's was all black, and Gavin's white with a brown mane. Gavin held on uneasily and glanced down, taking note of how far he was off the ground. Though the group looked completely harmless as armies go, sitting on the horses they at least felt the part.

Horace had been assigned to be the personal guard of the four youngest troops. Gavin called him their "platoon leader."

Nolan asked him, "Are there weapons in those two carts?"

"No. One's for our kitchen, and the other's tents."

"Shouldn't we have weapons?"

"There's no use in killin' Dreglings," Horace said. "There's more o' them than ye think."

"But shouldn't we have guns anyway, just in case?" asked Gavin.

"I warn ye, the Prince won't stand for it. Get it out of yer mind."

"But won't they try and kill us?"

"Maybe they would if they think yer goin' to kill them. Or if they think yer of no use. So look useful, gents, and it may save you yer skin. Vurmis would rather keep ye alive and have ye join him for his cause. But he can't control the Kingdom if he can't turn ye to his side."

Gavin asked, "Have you ever killed anyone?"

Horace paused. "I promise ye, there are many ways of killin' someone," he said softly, "but I try not to make a habit of it. Now, there'll be no more talk o' killin'."

"Still, I'd rather have something to defend myself," Nolan persisted.

Horace gave him a stern look, then spoke to both boys plainly and slowly. "It's not in the plan. The Prince knows what he's doin'. Trust him."

Prince Servan turned his horse to face his troops with final instructions before departing. "Stay with me," he said. "Follow my command. When you feel the greatest doubt, stay with me all the more. Stay with each other. There will be sorrow, and there will be happiness. But love, always love."

That was all he said. With Adwen at his side, Servan led his troops out through the castle gates without fanfare down to the docks on the bank of the river. They loaded horses, supplies, and themselves onto a ship that took them across the River Royal.

The trail up the Downfield River was wide, an easy start to the mission, but Gavin was feeling unsteady on his horse. Horace told him he was to ride behind his sister until he could get up enough confidence to ride by himself.

On the trail ahead of them, they saw Servan standing up in his stirrups, surveying the countryside at a slow trot. He was an encouraging sight on his grey dun, its black mane shimmering in the morning sun. Servan looked back and waved to the rest to move at a faster pace. The powerful movement of the horses beneath them was exhilarating. Analyse was completely in her element, and Gavin soon wanted to try riding by himself. His horse was so cooperative, practically all he had to do was hold on. They slowed to a strong, steady trot. It seemed the horses understood the Prince's plan better than anyone.

By late morning they came to a place Horace called the Darklands, and for good reason. Whatever human life may have inhabited the area at one time, it had died out long ago. All that remained were scraggly, dwarfed trees and a few shrubs on a gray barren landscape for as far as they could see. Ruins of homes sat in a state of decay. The land was hit so badly by the Plague, Horace said, that no one even remembered the original name of the place. They saw residue everywhere of the black poison they were already quite familiar with.

"This is creeping me out," Nolan said. "It's worse than Batty Woods."

"Exactly why the Prince wants us here," said Horace. "Places like this are the reason for this mission. So take a good look."

The black poison was so widespread they had to ride single file on a narrow trail. They could go neither right nor left without risking the horses stepping in the poisonous gunk. And they had come too far to turn back. Their only choice was straight ahead with the hush of death stalking all around them.

Nolan fidgeted, overcome by the odor of the place. Then, without warning, he suddenly jumped off his horse and ran. Adwen in the rear saw him first, dismounted, and caught Nolan by the arm. But Nolan had already gone one step too far into a shallow pool of black goo. He sat down on a stump and lifted his feet. The poison was already eating through the soles of his shoes.

Servan quickly removed Nolan's shoes and threw them aside. Someone pulled an extra pair of shoes from a backpack. Servan put them on Nolan's feet and helped him up onto his grey dun to ride double with him until he could recover his wits.

No one said anything as they moved forward. The silence of the Darklands was deafening. The palace, which had given them such comfort, now lay miles behind. At one point the Prince stopped to get their attention. He pointed to the sky and smiled. High above them, two eagles were soaring like escorts on their way.

Finally, two hours that seemed like twelve had passed when they rose out of the waste of the Darklands. They were entering the pristine beauty of lush, grass covered hills.

Soon a call went up from the front of the line. "Bounty Downs!" Everyone dismounted and sprawled out on a grassy slope along the trail. A breeze bowed the grass stems, and the grass whispered in unison, as if in homage to their royal company. It seemed to be consoling them, saying, "Rest, rest, sweet rest."

"I've been here before," Kate said to herself. This was the tranquil place, the exact place, that had come to her in her dreams more than once. The dreams had started sometime after her mom and dad began fighting. She had woken from the dream each time with a desire so intense that it made her cry. She would stare at her bedroom wall wondering where this place in her dream was and how she could reach it. During the daylight hours, that image of the hills would come to her sometimes without warning, and her sense of yearning would return.

Kate brushed her hand through the grass and held some to her face. Her dream was coming to life, and it seemed the dream had been preparing her for the Kingdom of What Is, for this moment.

Analyse asked, "What's up?"

"Nothing," Kate said. "I just know I'm really supposed to be here now. Somehow, this is where I was always meant to be."

The group pulled lunch items from their backpacks and ate. From where they sat in the peaceful, comforting Bounty Downs, it was hard to believe the Plague existed at all. Vurmis seemed like a bygone menace.

"Roots and jerky always tastes better in the outdoors," Nolan said sarcastically.

"And plums, of course," said Analyse, biting into one. She glanced down at Nolan's feet. "Uhm, nice shoes."

Kate and Analyse tried to hold in their laughter as Nolan gawked at his borrowed shoes. They were ones like those the early pilgrims wore, with large metal buckles instead of laces. Nolan snapped a picture of them with his phone, making them all burst into howls of laughter.

After lunch, Kate took out her map to add to it the palace, the depressing Darklands, and the hopeful Bounty Downs. A skein of geese flew over high in the blue sky. Kate watched them until they disappeared into the distance. Darklands or not, there would be no quick escapes on geese this time, she told herself.

Gavin and Nolan had walked off toward the top of the hill to explore just as Servan was calling everyone to take their last bites and prepare to move on.

"We'd better go get them," said Kate.

They started up the hill, searching for the boys. At the top they found them poking around an abandoned house, peeking through the windows. The girls stopped.

"You better knock it off, you guys," Analyse said. "Somebody might be living there."

Suddenly Nolan turned from the shed with terror in his eyes. "Run!" he yelled. "Dregs! Shadows!"

Chapter 18

Downfield

Analyse turned and ran down the hill, screaming, tripping, and rolling several times before she could stop herself. She looked back. Nolan stood at the top of the hill laughing.

"Did you really see Shadows, Nolan?" Gavin asked.

"It was a joke!" Nolan hollered down to Analyse on her hands and knees in the grass.

There were no Dreglings. The only shadows were their own, cast over the pristine hillside. Kate had not fallen for the prank and stood laughing at the spectacle of Analyse going head over heels, her red hair pinwheeling through the grass.

"My glasses!" screamed Analyse.

Somewhere in her tumble Analyse's glasses had come off. She searched futilely through the grass for several minutes. Finally, Nolan held up her glasses and said, "Did they look like this?"

Kate laughed until Analyse ran at Nolan and tackled him. She sat on him, swinging wildly with both fists. Nolan was laughing too hard to push her off. Suddenly, Analyse felt a large hand pulling her back. It was Horace. With his other hand he grabbed Nolan by the scruff of the neck.

"Enough of ye already!" Horace said. "If ye'd like to keep goin' at each other, we can either leave ye here, or we can have a visit with the Prince."

"She just attacked me," Nolan said.

"He stole my glasses!" she said, fumbling to put them back on.

"I didn't steal them. I found them right where you knocked them off."

"But you kept them. It's the same as stealing, dork, and then you mocked me!"

"It was just a joke."

Analyse came at him again, fists flying. Before she could land any punches, Horace pulled her back off.

"So, ye got it outa yer systems now?" Horace said. "Sit down, both of ye!" After they'd settled down, Horace said, "I'm hearin' accusations both ways. I'd say either yer both to blame or yer neither to blame. Which is it?"

Nolan wiped his nose, and Analyse caught her breath, not knowing how to respond to Horace's proposition.

"Well, talk it over," Horace said, "and let me know which one ye decide. For now, pull yerselves together because we've got bigger fish to fry than snipin' at each other. And for yer information, we don't joke about Shadows. The Prince won't stand for it. They're subjects of the Kingdom just the same as you and me."

As Horace was talking, Kate noticed a change in her friends' faces. Gaps had formed in Analyse's lips, and her teeth and gums were showing through. Also, Nolan's ears were cracking and coming apart. The lobe of one ear fell to the ground. Analyse and Nolan were in the early stages of disappearing, but neither seemed at all aware of what was happening to them. Kate was about to panic when Servan arrived.

Servan stood before Analyse and Nolan. They braced themselves for punishment, but the Prince did something unexpected. He took them by their chins and lifted their gaze to his own. Then he blew, long and gentle, onto their foreheads, first onto Analyse's then onto Nolan's, as if it were a ritual he'd had to perform many times before. As he did, Analyse's lips came back together and the pieces of Nolan's ears slowly reappeared and attached to one another. Lips and ears were being reconstituted.

Nolan and Analyse felt their flesh pulling together and put their hands to their ears and lips in bewilderment. In the end, the ordeal left only vague cracks in their skin as though their faces were dry from sun exposure.

"It's done," Servan said to them. "Now put it behind you. Look each other in the eye and shake hands."

They did as he said.

"We have to stay true to each other. We have a great challenge ahead," he told them.

Servan then blew on Kate's forehead also. Kate felt her lips tingling and put her hand up to discover cracks in her own lips. It had happened to her as well . . . and she understood why. Not only had she stood by when

Analyse, her best friend, was being hurt by being made the butt of a prank. She had also enjoyed it. They'd all been acting no better than Dreglings.

They left Bounty Downs behind, riding on a wide trail through hilly terrain. The horses felt stronger after the rest and some fresh grass. Servan called to let the horses gallop, which they did without hesitation. The horses' manes flew and their heads surged with each stride, thrilling their young riders. They would have loved to ride this way for the rest of the mission, but they had to conserve energy. There was still much ground to cover.

The troops paused outside a town called Downfield, which sat below them at the base of a shallow valley. Through its center ran the Downfield River, the same river that joined the River Royal near the palace. The river here was laced with ugly streaks of brown. With the wind blowing down river from the Great Gorge, the smoke gathered over the town, giving Downfield an eerie sepia aura. They detected a familiar stench. Evil hung in the air.

Downfield had been under Dregling control for decades, going back to the days of Vurmis's father, who had taken over the town at the start of the Rebellion and killed many of its people. Vurmis had put Downfield under the control of his right hand man, Feargus the Terrible, who had been with Vurmis from the start.

The town was an important stronghold for Vurmis. It was the last major town before reaching the Great Gorge. And from here Vurmis had access to everywhere else in the Kingdom. People had reported hearing frightening cries coming from Downfield over the years, so they normally gave the town a wide berth if they had to pass through the area.

Servan selected seven from the group to join him—Adwen, Kate, Analyse, Nolan, Gavin, and two women, Gail and Josephine. The others were to wait until they returned. Kate thought Josephine was a lot like her grandmother on her dad's side, strong and wise. She glanced at Kate with a twinkle in her eye as if she knew what Servan was up to.

"Stay with me," Servan said to his seven select troops. He calmly and confidently told them his plan. Gavin would leave his horse behind and ride double with Servan. Analyse would do the same with Josephine. Gail, Kate, Nolan, and Adwen would ride singly. Next, he told them to tear their clothes to make them look well-worn and pick up some mud to rub on their faces and arms. Anyone would assume them to be weary travelers, an extended family perhaps, looking for a place to rest. The ruse would gain them safe access to the Dregling leader, Feargus.

"And then we slit his throat?" Gavin inquired.

"No," Servan said, "We listen to his heart."

Gavin pulled up his nose and cocked his head to one side. The Prince put his hand on Gavin's shoulder to assure him his plan was the right one.

"Stay with me," Servan repeated.

Servan's idea was to beat the Dreglings at their own game, with deception. They would come as a poor family in need of help. With no more explanation, the group began their slow downward decent into the town.

They covered their noses as they passed several wooden edifices with bodies hanging from them. Dregling spies throughout the town had let nothing pass their leader's attention. When people were caught complaining about their Dregling masters or stealing anything, they were brought out and hung on the hillside in plain view of the town.

The spies took note of the haggard travelers on horseback approaching their town long before they arrived. The event of strangers coming into town, willingly and without being tricked into it, was unusual.

People gawked as they rode slowly through Downfield. Some were whole. Others were complete Shadows, and others had disappeared only partially—missing a hand, a leg, or portions of their heads. It was difficult not to appear shocked, but the people behaved as if they knew no other kind of life. Everything the people owned or earned went directly to Feargus the Terrible. Contrary to Vurmis's promises of happiness and wealth, the people were very poor.

Servan and his family were trying their best to fit the part of the downtrodden as they approached the town center. Feargus was waiting, having been given forewarning of their arrival. He greeted them with a broad gesture. Kate's heart went to her throat. Was this a signal for their execution?

"Welcome!" Feargus announced as Servan dismounted and bowed, completely at ease.

Feargus wore heavy black boots and a long red silk jacket elaborately embroidered in gold. He had gone almost completely to shadow. The upper half of his head was absent, leaving only his mouth and jaws, and when he spoke, Kate noticed he had no teeth or tongue. His mouth was a vacant hole from which his voice came hollow and dark. He had no hands. Where his fingers should have been were several jeweled rings that sparkled in the sun.

Feargus said, "You and your family needn't have any worry. We will provide for you here. In time, if you work hard, and if all goes well, each of you may become a part of my most honored inner circle." Searching for a reaction, he added, "This means you will enjoy the wealth of the land and have as much as you want."

"Your generosity is impressive if only this was yours to grant," Servan said and concentrated for a moment as if looking directly into the Dregling's heart. "I know you never wanted all of this, Feargus."

Feargus cast him a threatening glare from eyes that were not there. Servan did not flinch, and the longer he looked at Feargus, the more perplexed Feargus appeared.

"You've been made leader of this town," said Servan.

"Appointed first lieutenant by the great Grod Vurmis," Feargus confirmed defensively.

"But it has cost you dearly."

Feargus steeled his jaw. Servan's horse shifted nervously beside him. Servan stroked his neck to calm him.

"You've been lonely most of your life," Servan told him. "You were only twelve when your father died in the Rebellion fighting against what you now represent. Back then, kids envied you for the way you could invent toys and gadgets out of scraps of wood."

Feargus's cavernous mouth opened in horror. "How do you know—?"

"I knew you when we were school boys in the same school, working to do our best. The other kids bullied you. They mocked and belittled you because you were different, and they stole the little toys you created. I tried to stop them, but they continued tormenting you."

Feargus gaped, finally recognizing him. "Booker?" He searched Servan's face for some memory of the schoolboy he once knew.

Servan said, "You never knew how to answer back to those bullies, because they diminished you. They stole from you the most precious thing you had—your voice. I remember the sadness of that young boy."

It was as though a curtain parted from the Dregling's face. No one had ever spoken to him like this. His eyes began to form where they had once existed long ago.

"Then one day, Vurmis came," Servan continued. "He promised you a voice in exchange for your life. He was your only hope. He would give you Downfield, and you would serve him as his right hand man. People who once insulted you would now have to listen to you. But what Vurmis gave you was not really your voice. It was *his* voice. And he's been using it all these years to keep these people as slaves."

Feargus's lips trembled as his mouth opened to say something, but no words came out. Gradually a tongue formed in disjointed pieces, appearing like partially chewed toast. As he tried frantically to speak, shocked at what was happening to him, his teeth clattered in his mouth like a jumble of M&M's. Finally, his entire face appeared, patched and worn, in the early stage of reconstituting itself.

Kate held her hands over her mouth and nose as she wondered if anyone else saw or smelled what she did. Spirits of Dreglings were streaming from Feargus's mouth, screaming in anguish and flying away as though released from a deep dungeon. With them rose an awful stench, far worse even than the smell of burnt hair.

His men tried to pick Feargus up from the ground, embarrassed to see their master in such a humiliated state, but Feargus pushed them away. The men rushed on Servan.

"No," Feargus said, motioning for his men to back off.

Servan bent down and whispered into his ear, "Love . . . only love."

Feargus clung to Servan's arm. "Who are you!" he cried. "Tell me what to do, or else leave me and never return!"

"You'll not stay here any longer. You will stay with me. Mount your horse. We have one last battle."

"Battle? Tell me plainly what you want with me," Feargus pleaded.

"Come with us to the Great Gorge."

"I . . . I cannot."

"But you must. We will defeat Grod Vurmis together."

Feargus protested, "He'll throw me into his furnace."

"And if you continue what you're doing, you will only be dying a long and terrible death here. Either you must come, or you'll never be free. You don't need to fear Vurmis any longer. His end is near, and his little kingdom will end with him."

With Adwen and Servan's help, Feargus finally stood up.

Servan put a hand on Feargus's shoulder. "Your name is no longer Feargus the Terrible. Your name is Feargus Friend of Servan."

Feargus turned to him in shock. It finally came to him who had rescued him—Prince Servan himself. His heart fragile and broken, he removed his rings and his red jacket, dropped them where he stood, and sobbed. It was a cry of remorse for wasted years, a cry of happiness and freedom, all at once. Servan removed his own coat and wrapped it around him.

A peace and gentleness that was much stronger than the blustering Dregling had come over Feargus. Just as with Mirabelle, the foul odour left him. Now came the smell, perhaps one from his childhood, of fresh cut cedar.

Feargus looked around at the men that had served as his hands and feet in Downfield, delivering death and oppression. He ordered them to step down, disband, and relinquish control of the city. They would no longer hold the city or its people captive.

The men turned and ran, some in fear and others as though a terrible weight had been lifted from them.

When the people of the town saw Feargus leaving on his horse with Servan and his humble troops, they stopped in their tracks and dropped what they were doing. Workers stopped unloading goods, merchants left their shops, and police stopped patrolling the streets as they saw their leader riding out of town.

Servan paused to speak to the people. "From this day forward, this town belongs to the King," he shouted. "You are free!" His voice echoed down the streets and over the rooftops into every crevice of the town.

"Free, everyone free!" Feargus repeated. It was clear he spoke not only of Downfield but of himself. And his words were the truest he had ever spoken.

The people gazed at their hands and feet and at each other. Over the next several days, the air was filled with an incessant popping and crackling while their bodies came back together. The sound of flesh healing was so relentless at times that people could not sleep because of the noise. But there were no complaints. People lay in bed giggling, giddy with the astonishing realization that they and their neighbors were regaining their truer selves.

The news spread how Servan had, without so much as a sword, taken their leader. And the oppression they'd known like a filthy smog for so long began to lift. The people turned their faces down river toward the palace and smiled as a crisp, cool breeze blew over the town from the north. The air began to clear.

Over the next days, the people of Downfield would on occasion whistle to themselves for no apparent reason, tunes they thought they'd long forgotten. They would spontaneously begin dancing whenever some music started up, and embrace each other on the street whenever they felt like it. For the first time in years they were telling the old stories, one person filling in gaps that the other had forgotten, another starting up a new story, all of them laughing and crying and feeling a kind of love they had never known.

Some had recognized Prince Servan while he was there briefly that day, and eventually over the ensuing days the entire town had heard the news that it was him.

The forces who had been waiting on the hill heard the cheers coming from the valley. They saw the yellowish tinge in the sky clearing and felt the cooling wind. They cheered loudly as they saw Servan and their fellow troops coming with Feargus among them. Gavin, proud to be among the conquerors, raised his fist to the sky.

Chapter 19

An Elite Task Force

The night of Downfield's liberation, Servan and his troops made camp in the hills above the town. Sounds of celebration erupted from the valley throughout the night. In the bushes around camp, they could hear movement. "Listen," Servan said. "Squirrels—they're celebrating too!"

Kate, Analyse and Gavin could not sleep, thinking about the day's events. So Servan stayed up with them and told stories—one funny one about a family of dancing squirrels that came out at a full moon to entertain the other animals. They finally nodded off. Servan covered them with blankets and was so exhausted he also fell asleep on the spot.

Downfield now posed a major obstacle for Vurmis. His easiest path from the Great Gorge to the rest of the Kingdom was lost. Vurmis and his Dreglings would have to take much more difficult routes to spread their influence, through thick forests and over mountainous terrain.

The victory did not, however, stop the flow of poison in the Downfield River from the Great Gorge to the River Royal. Grod Vurmis the worm was still feeding his voracious appetite for more and more of the land, all toward his one goal—to build his own empire and take over What Is.

As they rode into the mountains toward the Great Gorge, the thought of what lay ahead weighed heavily on Servan. Bowed over his horse, he seemed to age several decades before their eyes. His hair had gone gray, blending him in with the color of his horse. His body swayed slightly with each step up the stony trail, the destiny of the Kingdom on his shoulders.

Servan paused at a spot that offered a clear view looking back. The Downfield River snaked toward its junction with the River Royal.

Gavin pointed to a spot along the River Royal. "There!"

In the distance behind them, the palace lay glistening in the bend of the river like a baby in the crook of a mother's arm. Its terracotta facade stood out brightly in the mid-day sun. Servan sat up tall again, receiving encouragement from the sight of the palace. The horses also responded in kind with confident steps. Servan's grey dun's ears twitched, alert to every sound.

The troops were entering steeper terrain. The carts at one point had to be unloaded, lifted by hand over a bolder field, and then reloaded again. They would ride in the protection of the trees all the way to the mouth of the Great Gorge. There they would camp and take stock before the final assault.

Feargus had traveled the valley many times and wisely advised Servan to follow a lesser used trail that Dreglings rarely used. His advice saved them from being discovered. Twice along the way, they heard voices and horses passing below them close to the river on the main trail. Feargus recognized the voices immediately as Dreglings, coming down from the Great Gorge.

"They'll have a little surprise when they get to Downfield," Feargus said with a smile.

As the valley grew narrower, the river ran faster, and the yellow filth it carried grew thicker. Though they could not see it, they could smell it. At one time in the distant past, the people of this area had drunk straight from the river. But now, instead of the white spray of its rapids, it threw up chunks of discarded debris from Vurmis's foundries.

The stillness of the mountains was hypnotizing. Heads nodded sleepily, some dozed, as they rode back and forth on switchbacks. Josephine looked up through the spruce trees, which had lost most of their needles from the Plague, leaving only spindles of branches stretching into the pale yellow sky.

"Awake!" Josephine cried.

Horses and their riders startled at her voice. Servan stopped the line.

"This dozing is a deception of the enemy," she announced, her voice echoing through the forest. "He makes the land gray with death in hopes it will lull us all to sleep while his own head swells with confidence. A great battle lies ahead of a kind the Kingdom has never before seen. Wake, and prepare."

Josephine spoke more words in guttural tones of the traditional tongue. She looked as if some unexpectedly dark horror had revealed itself to her. She repeated softly over and over, "*Wagenchka, wagenchka . . .*"

Kate looked over to Horace, puzzled.

"*Wagenchka,*" he sighed. "Have mercy."

Mercy for what, Kate didn't dare to ask. Nor did anyone else ask as they solemnly pushed ahead, meditating on Josephine's words.

Late in the afternoon, the valley finally widened out again over a broad plain. It was an area called simply The Farms. It had been the home of several productive farms at one time, but now the landscape showed the same signs of decay they had seen in the Darklands. Crusty black patches lay over the fields, where the poison had hardened over a period of time. Surprisingly, the people in the area were carrying on and trying to make the best of their situation.

The troops paused as Servan called the royal greeting at the gate of one house. A couple edged their way out of a barn, tools in hand, then relaxed at the sight of Servan and ran forward to greet them.

"Hello, Scythehelder," said the Prince.

Scythehelder had news. Dreglings were coming from the Gorge and convincing more and more people of The Farms to sell all their produce to Vurmis at half the going rate. They threatened that if the locals didn't go in with Vurmis, he would finish off their beloved farms inch by inch.

Servan encouraged him to hang on for a couple more days. Scythehelder offered Servan what little food they had and showed him the best place to set up camp.

The stench here was constant. Less than an hour lay between them and the Great Gorge. It was nearly dark, but the smog was so thick it was difficult to tell if the sun was really setting and the day nearly ended. They set up a base camp, pitching tents at the edge of a wooded area, where they would be less conspicuous. Kate and Analyse had no sooner finished putting up their tent when they saw Adwen approaching with someone they recognized—Grover.

"I was told I might find you here!" Grover said with a wide smile, parting his dark beard with a row of white teeth. The girls did not expect to see him on the mission, and now they were as delighted as two kids getting a surprise visit from their favorite uncle.

"How—" Kate began.

"It was in the plan, but I couldn't tell you. A few weeks ago, I was just falling asleep when I heard a strange call in the grove. It was an owl. But instead of the normal 'who! who! who!' it was calling 'you! you! you!'"

Kate and Analyse stared in disbelief and laughed.

"No joke," Grover continued. "That's what they said. So I went out to check, and sure enough, the owl had a message that I would be on this mission, but no details about when and how. Until two days ago, when another message came with details from you-know-hoo-hoo, King Athar. And here I am."

The girls were delighted to be reunited with their confident, caring friend.

Grover pointed to a high ridge with a saddle shaped dip at its top. "I came over Saddle Pass. That was the short but hard way. I suggest you never try it."

Grover was eager to hear about their journey. He raised his eyebrows, captivated and full of questions about Bowman and their voyage up the River Royal.

"The King and Queen are more amazing than we could have imagined," Kate said, "and the palace—it's beautiful, and—"

"And the library—" Analyse interrupted. "If you think *you've* got a lot of books, you should see this, it's huge—and they gave us horses—"

"And the Queen, she took me to meet this woman Mirabelle, and she told me her story, her whole story."

They told Grover about the Darklands and Downfield and Feargus Friend of Servan, recounting events so fast their words could not keep up.

"I told Aster that you two could do it," Grover said finally, "and I was right. I'm proud of you. And by the way, we'll be putting your stories in the Royal Library."

"Nobody knows for sure what we do when we reach the Gorge," said Analyse, worried.

"And neither do I," Grover said with a smile. "Servan knows. I do know he wants me to do something before the Gorge, which may involve you, I'm told."

Grover held up a book. The title was *A Brief Chronology of Stories, Kingdom or Otherwise, in Pictorial Form: From North, South, East, West, Up, Down, and Beyond.*

"If only the title were as brief as the chronology," Grover said and leafed through the book of only some thirty pages with images of petroglyphs.

"We will hopefully be adding to this account. But this book helps explain the most common pictorial representations—that we know of. I've apparently been selected as the expert on engravings in stone—mythical or real. Certain images carry universal significance, sometimes transcendent, the importance of which—"

Grover stopped, noticing the girls screwing up their faces.

"Can you give us the brief version?" Analyse asked.

"Okay . . . basically, uhm, we're supposed to try to find out what Vurmis's pictures in stone say. The book is simply interesting and, I hope, helpful."

"We saw some petroglyphs by the caves."

"In the caves and in the cliffs, yes. It's the way Vurmis is communicating to his people about his own importance, about his intentions, and what have you. Now—"

Adwen approached the huddle of non-stop storytellers, holding up a grouse and two rabbits. "You get a break from roots and jerky tonight. We managed to get these, and Scythehelder gave us a goat. We'll feast."

They did feast on succulent rabbit stew and roast grouse. They had turnips and spinach from the farms. The goat was turned slowly on a spit over the campfire to a tenderness that could make a hardened vegetarian swoon in ecstasy from the way the meat fell off the bone. More of everything remained after everyone had seconds. After a long, difficult day with minimal sustenance, the color was returning to everyone's faces. The taste of fresh food brought laughter and singing to the camp.

Servan sat down with Grover, Kate, and Analyse as they lingered over their last bites of dinner.

"The King and Queen and I have agreed on a vital task for the three of you," Servan began. "We feel you make the best team for what we are needing right now."

They were to be scouts. Tomorrow morning they would be going to the caves in the cliffs above the Great Gorge. Servan believed Vurmis and his scribes had been etching propaganda there and possibly leaving details of their plan. Their job was to decipher as much as they could and bring back what they found. It would be a challenging climb, and they would have to go by a less frequent route so they would not raise suspicion.

The girls felt overwhelmed to be selected for such an elite task, and to be going with Grover was a chance they would never pass up.

"Grover is a master of stories and pictures," Servan said, "but young people often catch things older people miss. You have an acute perception and intuition, Kate. You see with a third eye as we say—deeper meanings, the bigger picture, things beyond the surface. And, Analyse, your intellect for someone so young is exceptional."

The girls blushed at such high praise from the Prince.

"What about Gavin and Nolan?" Kate asked.

"They've got important jobs also," said Servan, "which I've already gone over with them."

Kate was too excited that night to fall asleep. Finally she slipped over the threshold into a deep, contented sleep.

The next thing the girls noticed was a tapping on their shoulders at the tent opening. It was Grover telling them it was time to go. Their heads still fuzzy with sleep, they pulled their gear together for their journey to the caves. They grabbed a couple of bites of leftover grouse and made sure their water containers were full. It was still dark. Everyone else was sound asleep as they made their way through a scattering of tents. A cow bawled in the distance and farm tools clanged.

They had walked only a few minutes from base camp when they looked up and saw the cliffs looming above them and a series of holes near the top—their destination. The Prince wanted them back to camp by midday the next day. They would have a lot of work to do in a short time.

The girls described to Grover, with as much detail as they could, the carvings they'd discovered on their first visit to the cliffs.

"Good," said Grover. "That information will help when we put it together with the other petroglyphs we find."

Within an hour they were already halfway to the caves. They were following a trail that was at points no wider than three feet with a steep drop to their left. Suddenly Analyse screamed when she lost her footing on a loose rock. Her pack swayed, and she lost her balance. Her feet slipped over the edge, and she clung with her upper body draped across the path but unable to get a grip on anything. Kate grabbed her arm to stop her from slipping further but could not pull her up. Grover had gone ahead but hurried back when he heard screams. Just as Kate was losing her grip, Analyse felt a nudge on her buttocks from below.

"Come on, I'm not doing everything myself," said a voice below. "Keep pulling while I push."

In an instant Analyse was shoved back onto the trail. Scrambling up to join her were two mountain goats.

"We saw that one coming," one of them said. "Next time, hire a goat or two *before* starting the climb."

The girls sat on the trail, beside themselves with amazement. They'd lost track of how often they'd been rescued by the timely acts of animals, not to mention humans, during their time in What Is.

Servan's three scouts started up the trail again, but now their way was made easier by two goats pushing the girls from behind. At moments they were almost floating up the trail. The first goat lowered her head and gave Kate a big push that made her skip a step. "There, that's goat truth," the goat said.

A couple hundred feet ahead was the first cave.

"This is as far as we go," said one goat. "Those caves are out of our providence."

The three walkers thanked the goats.

"Don't thank us," one replied. "Just pass on a request to the King, or whoever's in charge these days. Ask if it would be too much trouble for us to have just one or two of those caves, ones that haven't been trashed or taken over, I mean. Nothing big and elaborate necessary, mind you, just a couple of the teeny little ones would be fine. Kind of slim pickings around here."

They promised they would relay the message. Grover assured the goats that things were about to change. With that, the shaggy, very capable, rescue duo took their leave and tiptoed over the edge of the trail with a nibble-footedness seen only among their kind.

The trail flattened to a ledge, and the ledge soon widened by several feet, where they found three caves. Debris and charred wood from a fire was scattered around the opening of one cave, which was probably a temporary shelter for Dreglings, Grover said.

As they looked over the ledge to the canyon, lumps caught in the girls' throats. There was the Great Gorge, but remarkably changed from the last time they'd seen it. The sight was breathtaking in a most terrible way. There were now two furnaces. And looming from the bottom of the Gorge to the top of the surrounding cliffs, eye-level with them, was a magnificent tower like nothing they had ever witnessed.

Chapter 20

The Caves

The tower had a square base and nine or ten tiers with staircases between them. It narrowed at its top to a small shrine with stone pillars and a dome cover inlaid with gemstones and diamonds that sparkled brightly. Around the base of the tower and on it, hundreds of workers were hauling stones in hoists while others were setting the stones and sealing them in place with mortar. Among the workers were people in red robes, pacing and keeping workers in line. In the shrine at the top Kate thought she could make out a man and woman and two large, decorated thrones. The man was leaning out observing the construction.

"They're making some kind of pyramid," Analyse said.

Grover said, "Yes, a pyramid, perhaps a temple, and those people in red I'm guessing are priests."

"And the two people at the top?" Kate asked, shuddering at what the answer may be.

"The prince of evil himself, I would expect, with a woman he's likely chosen to be his queen, or goddess, of his empire."

The Gorge was also wider. Vurmis had quarried the stone for the tower from the far wall of the Gorge until it looked like a block of cheese chewed by rodents from the inside out. Vurmis was expanding his center of operations. On the far side of the Gorge were piles of stone where another building project, long and rectangular, was in its beginning stages.

Smoke billowed from the two large furnaces, which they could now see were a kind of foundry. People were feeding charcoal into the furnaces through thick iron doors while others were working bellows to keep the fire hot. Outside the furnaces lay piles of iron beams that could be used for construction.

"He's found some methods for building we haven't seen before," Grover said. "Nothing of this size and sophistication exists anywhere else in the Kingdom."

The large pool of the yellow-white poison at the bottom of the Gorge had grown also, and now it was divided into several smaller pools with walkways like dikes between them. Dreglings were dipping from the pools and pouring the poison into vats and loading the vats on carts.

"That must be how they get the Plague to other places," said Analyse.

"It also makes a good defence," said Grover. "Any army coming up this valley toward the tower—it would be treacherous. They would be stopped in their tracks by the jigsaw of walkways and poisonous pools."

A worker screamed as one of the vats of poison tipped from its cart and spilled over him. The others ignored him and placed the vat back on the cart and carried on. The man lay writhing in pain until he suddenly stopped moving. One of the men in red pointed, and two workers ran to the fallen man. With one foot each, they rolled his body into the pond.

Near the top of the tower at three locations were cables, stretching from the topmost tier below the shrine to the tops of the surrounding cliffs.

"Looks like suspension bridges," Grover said. "It makes it much easier for them to get out of here and go to other parts of the Kingdom. So they have backup routes even though the way through Downfield is cut off. We need to take all this back to Servan."

Grover was impressed though not fearful, but the girls' hearts sank. The size of the tower made the palace look like a dollhouse. They would be no match against this, even with a thousand more troops, armed and trained.

Analyse went pale. "I didn't sign up for this," she mumbled.

"You're right," said Grover, "the King and Queen signed you up. You'll have a chance to turn back later if you want. For now, we have a job to do."

After the girls had gathered their wits, they followed Grover to one cave that extended deep into the cliff. Before going in, Grover made a small fire and removed several chunks of wax from his pack, which he melted in a can over the fire. He took three sticks, wound some rope around each one, and dipped these into the melted wax.

"Torches," he said. "Essential for cave exploration, but they don't last forever. So remember, however deep we go in, we have to find our way back again."

When the wax had dried, they each took one torch, lit it, and stepped inside the cave. It was musty and damp. They were surprised to find how high the ceiling was. Filaments of moisture seeped down the rock surface like a mass of wet yarn. They slowly examined the walls.

"What exactly are we looking for?" asked Analyse.

"Petroglyphs of any kind or any kind of script, something that might tell us the locations of villages Vurmis has taken, or wants to take, anything that may tell us details about The Worm's plan. Anything that looks unusual." His voice echoed through the cave. The light of his torch on his bushy head made gargoyle shapes on the walls.

Kate held something heavy in her hand. "What is this?"

"*Grith afal!*" Grover gasped. "Shackles. They've been using them for their slaves."

Kate immediately dropped them and screamed, wiping her hands on her pants.

They heard the sound of dripping water from somewhere in the cave and moved toward it.

"What do you make of this?" asked Grover, passing his finger tips over a figure carved in the wall. There was not just one petroglyph. The entire wall was covered with pictures like graffiti. Kate noticed what appeared to be a map, including markings of key locations. Under each of these markings was writing that Kate could not make out.

"What does this say?"

Grover inspected it closely and sighed. "Vurmis is using the ancient language so that only a trained few can read his plan. This says 'captured' under each of these locations. They're towns controlled by Dreglings. We already know about some of them, but these villages here . . . " He put his finger on four or five dots. "I had no idea. This is much more extensive than anyone thought."

There was despair in his voice that told of much loss. His finger came to rest on one dot at the edge of the map. "This is where Aster's parents live. We haven't heard from them in weeks. Perhaps now we know why. In all of these places people are going to need help if it's not already too late."

"Over here!" Analyse's voice echoed from deeper in the cave.

Analyse stood in front of a long row of books set on a bench. It was an alcove, like a small reading area with ten or so seats in a circle.

"It's like a little school," she said.

Grover picked up a couple of the books. "This looks like part of Vurmis's library. He's replacing the old stories with these," he said, paging through one. "Clever. He's using the ancient language to make his stories look more authentic. Why, I'm not sure, but he may be trying to control his message . . . by putting the stories in the hands of only a few people who are learned in the old language . . . and then making these people his mouthpiece. Whatever the case, it's an elaborate effort to brainwash everyone. This is probably a work area where his scribes have been writing."

"What do these lines mean?" Kate said, pointing to a series of dashes on the wall arranged in a descending pattern toward the back of the cave. Over these dashes were carved random letters within squares.

Grover was stumped. "It's a code for something," he said. "But codes are usually in the old language, and these are not." He examined them for another minute. "The letters . . . the images . . . they don't add up to anything."

They were ready to start back when Kate said suddenly, "Exactly, they don't mean anything!"

"What are you saying?"

"The letters in the squares—they're not meant to say anything! They're books. See? And the dashes are stairs." She traced her finger along the row of dashes, which were equally spaced, each a little lower than the one before it.

"I get it," said Analyse. "The dashes all go down in one direction, and they point to the back of the cave."

"Stairs . . . with books!" Kate nearly shouted. "He probably has books from the Royal Library back there."

Grover said, "I think you're on to something. Well done."

Following this clue, Kate took a few steps to the back of the cave.

"There's stairs over here!" she said.

A stone staircase went gradually down. They followed it cautiously. Their torches flickered in a draft coming from below. In the draft they detected two distinct odours. The first Analyse recognized immediately as the musty smell of old books. The other smell was foul, but they couldn't make it out.

At the bottom of the steps was a large metal door, which was unlocked. The three of them put their shoulders into the door, and it opened with a loud metallic groan. They stepped into a room so large their lights could barely make out the far end, where there appeared to be an opening leading further back into the cave.

They took a few more steps and paused. The floor was stained with large red blotches. Around the periphery of the room were three-foot crevices in the wall. The foul odour was now so strong they had to cover their noses. Then they recognized what it was—dog feces. A moment later, there was a horrific chorus of snarling and barking. Four large dogs barged out of the crevices, their fangs glistening in the torch light.

"Go back," Grover ordered, "run!" He pushed the girls back up the stairs. When the girls reached the mouth of the cave, they looked back gasping. Grover was not with them. After a minute of panic, he finally emerged, limping badly, and fell to the ground. His leg was bleeding. He took a knife from his pack and cut away his pant leg to expose his leg, badly mangled. He tore strips from a spare shirt and guided the girls in applying a bandage to contain the bleeding.

"What were those dogs?" Kate asked.

"Moorhounds," Grover said, groaning. "Cross wolves with large dogs, and you get moorhounds—more vicious than a common guard dog. He uses them to guard his possessions . . . or Kingdom possessions, as the case may be. He's probably got a whole collection of stolen books down there. Judging by the blood on the floor, he might be using the hounds to carry out torture there too."

"What do we do now?" Kate asked.

"This leg doesn't look good. I won't be able to explore any more caves, we'll have to go back with what we have." He tried to get up, grimacing with each step, and sat back down.

They would have to get him back to camp to be cared for properly. They found a stick he could use as a crutch, but they'd gone no more than ten minutes before he had to sit down again.

"This won't work," he said. "We'll need a pull sled."

Following Grover's instructions, the girls found four solid, straight tree branches. They placed the two longest ones side by side about two feet apart. The two shorter ones they placed across these to form a square while Grover tied them in place. Then he cut a portion of his blanket and stretched it across the square. Using rope, he tied the blanket securely in place to form a seat.

Kate and Analyse looked at each other, expecting the next instructions to be for each to grab the end of a pole and start pulling, but Grover had a different idea.

"We'll need one of those goats again," he said.

He held his hands to his mouth and gave a bleating call that sounded exactly like a goat. After another call, a goat appeared above them.

It came tiptoeing down the rock face to where Grover sat in the seat of his newly made pull sled. Seeming to know exactly what was required, the goat positioned itself between the two extended poles. Grover told the girls how to harness the goat in with rope.

The moment of truth came as he sat himself in the seat. It held beautifully. The goat could pull him with ease as they started downhill.

They hadn't gone far when they heard voices behind them in the area of the caves. This was the only nudge they needed to start moving faster. The goat walked so quickly that by the time they reached camp, the girls were exhausted from trying to keep up.

Everyone was surprised to see them a full day ahead of schedule. Grover was disappointed and not in good shape. He would have to stay at the Scythehelder's farm and miss the rest of the mission to the Great Gorge. But he and the girls offered some valuable information.

Servan shook his head at the mention of shackles and moorhounds and the suffering this must have meant for Vurmis's captives. With the information about captured villages, Servan decided to send back two from the group to the palace with the news. Ships would be sent to the towns on Vurmis's map to take them back under the King's rule.

Servan had some sad news for Kate—Gavin had been captured by Dreglings. He and Nolan had been sent for fresh water from a nearby well, and as they were filling containers, a couple of farmers offered to help carry the water back to camp. Nolan was walking ahead, and when he turned around, Gavin and the two farmers were gone.

Nolan was distraught and did not dare to face Kate, who was overcome with anxiety and guilt that she had left him. What were they going to do with him? How would she tell her mom and dad?

"Come on!" she screamed hysterically. "We have to get him back. Now!"

Kate began running up the trail toward the plume of smoke rising above the Gorge. She'd gone a hundred feet when Adwen and Feargus caught up to her and brought her back to camp.

"But they'll kill him!" Kate cried, kicking.

"We'll get him back, I promise," said Servan. "But we'll do it together."

He held Kate to give her a chance to calm down before he spoke again. "Gavin will be at the Great Gorge when we get there. He's a fighter. He won't give in easily to Vurmis."

"I know he's a fighter," cried Kate. "He'll sass them, and they'll kill him!"

Chapter 21

The Final Assault

F inding her brother consumed Kate's every thought. For the rest of the day, she could eat nothing and do nothing.

Josephine took Kate aside and walked with her and told her own story—how she was once captured by Dreglings and how she escaped. She had been in the Gorge for ten days and thought she'd never make it out, she said. And now here she was as part of Servan's special forces.

"Gavin will not give in to Vurmis because he's lived with Servan," Josephine said. "Like me. I couldn't turn away and forget the Prince. It's like fresh water—you just keep coming back to it because you can never forget the taste. When Vurmis saw I wasn't going to give in, he just yelled at me to get out of his sight he was so sick of me," she laughed. "He assumed I'd never make it back to Servan alive. Well, he had another guess coming. We'll get Gavin back, don't worry."

When Servan heard that stolen Kingdom books were probably hidden in the caves, he was not surprised. They would eventually take them back, but first things first. Taking down Vurmis and his stronghold were Servan's only focus. But the extent of Vurmis's following and what he had done in the Gorge visibly shook the Prince. He took Adwen aside, and the two considered what lay ahead. He wanted reassurance of the rightness of his plan, and he knew his trusted friend would be honest with him.

The rumor around camp was that the King and Queen would be sending large reinforcements to join them, enough to overcome Grod Vurmis and his forces. The news raised the morale of the group. They knew they'd done the hard ground work of reclaiming Downfield, scouting ahead, and setting up a forward camp. Now, the only thing needed was a good assault plan with overwhelming force. They were confident the Prince would soon lay out the plan and make everything clear. They waited anxiously. Now and then someone scouted back down the valley, looking for the reinforcements.

But as darkness approached, no one else had arrived.

When Servan heard what the troops were thinking, he had to dispel immediately any notion of reinforcements. None would be coming. They already had what they needed to defeat Vurmis, he said. If they just stuck with the King's plan, they would be victorious. Gavin would be saved, along with many others who had not seen their families for years.

But some of troops did not believe him. They thought they detected some uncertainty in the Prince. Arguing erupted, beginning with one or two voices, followed by others.

They were only twenty plus in number, they argued to Servan . . . they were not equipped . . . they were untrained . . . they would be easily overtaken . . . they could even be killed. Some offered to go on a recruiting mission for more troops.

Someone accused Feargus of being a spy, and a scuffle broke out.

"This man is responsible for good people dying—thousands! And now he's leading us into a trap! Once a Dregling, always one! We should have hung him in the town square."

Others joined in the accusations and forced Feargus to the ground. Someone called on Servan to give them the word.

"We kill him now, or we'll be killed ourselves!"

Servan ordered them to let him go, and they all stood.

"How many of you were once Dreglings?" he said.

There was silence. Many of them had been, including those who were calling for Feargus to die.

"You should be standing proud," the Prince continued. "You are the special forces of the King. You've been called on to take back the Kingdom. Not because you've been such good citizens—you've all failed in your past. But the King has personally chosen you for this task."

Adwen faced the troops and spoke. "You have a choice. You can return home, or you can stand with the Prince and be a part of the greatest day the Kingdom has ever known. Leave and you will have no part in this victory."

After a minute's deliberation, only seven out of the twenty-three troops stepped forward to join Servan—Adwen, Feargus, Horace, Josephine, Kate, Analyse, and Nolan. They were a humble assembly without weapons. Kate wondered whether they were just stupid to think they could take on an enemy like Vurmis in his tower.

Nothing else was said. Those who did not step forward were allowed to leave whenever they wanted to. Those who had thrown their lot in with the Prince would be setting out early the next day.

That night, Kate slipped in and out of sleep. She heard coyotes howling in the distance, a mournful, lonely sound. In a half-sleep, she saw the cougar's eyes in Batty Woods. This was immediately followed by the image of Kayla, then Mirabelle, Feargus, and Gavin in quick succession, like a slideshow of Vurmis's victims.

At seeing Gavin's face in her sleep, Kate bolted awake, breathless, trying to remember Josephine's comforting words. She finally went back to sleep, and her dream continued. She saw them all again. They were looking down into a hole, a square pit hewn in rock. Rose petals were scattered over the bottom. As they looked, the floor of the pit began to rise until it became a square table around which they all sat, with Prince Servan joining them. On the table before them were bowls of royal trifle.

When Kate woke, she felt surprisingly confident and at peace in her choice to go with Servan. No one else had changed his or her mind either. Many had packed up and gone back home in the night. The number standing with Servan was still seven.

They would ride under darkness before dawn. They would leave their gear and take with them only water and a few bites of food.

Nolan was assigned to carry the royal flag. It was important, Servan said, that he keep it held up under all circumstances, especially as they approached the tower of Grod Vurmis. It had to be clear that they came in the name of the King and Queen.

Kate and Analyse were given a record book, like a notebook. They were to observe events carefully and write down what they saw and heard. There could be no doubt anywhere in the land about what had happened on this day. They could rely on others' input, but they were ultimately the ones responsible for putting everything in the record for this and future generations.

The horses were restless, sensing the final assault was near. Servan's grey dun reared and snorted and pranced anxiously, eager to get on with the battle.

Servan led them steadily up the main trail to the Great Gorge. Their only light was the dim glow of dawn above the cliffs. A couple of eagles soared over the Gorge ahead. Finally, as they rounded an outcropping of rock, there it loomed—Vurmis's immense tower, menacing, itself a shadow in the darkness of the Great Gorge. The shrine at its top rose just high enough above the rim of the Gorge to give a wide view of the Kingdom for miles. It's gem covered dome caught the early morning sun, setting off sparks—red, green, and white—like flashing spears.

Why Vurmis had chosen this place as his lair was obvious. Not only was it hidden in a deep gorge high in the mountains, but it was also protected by the abrupt cliff walls on three sides. And it could not be approached except by coming up the canyon on this trail or coming across one of the suspension bridges from the rim to the tower.

Nolan pointed out that a gorge was also an easy place for them to get trapped. He rode his horse up next to Horace with an idea. "Send me to the tower as a spy. I can pretend I'm a Dregling, and when I get inside, I'll find Gavin and we'll escape."

"This is not in the Prince's plan. Stay quiet," Horace said.

They stopped at a massive pile of boulders within three hundred feet of the furnaces. No Dreglings were anywhere in sight. Not even sentries were posted. On the rim of the Gorge, hundreds of crows were perched, along with a herd of deer, their ears pointed forward, like an audience to the event. Vurmis was apparently feeling very confident not to have guards posted in their way. The troops dismounted and left their horses hidden behind the boulders.

"I need your eyes," Servan said to everyone. "Go there onto that pile of boulders to the left. Adwen will come with me. Stay and watch until Adwen gives you the order."

"What order?" Nolan muttered as they climbed to their lookout, their hearts pounding.

"What are we watching for?" Analyse said.

"We'll all find out soon enough," said Horace.

Servan and Adwen moved forward on foot, finding their way through the labyrinth of poisonous pools toward the tower as the others moved to the top of the hill.

Nolan laid down his flag momentarily to take some pictures, which he thought was sensible as part of "watching."

"Evidence," he told Kate. "We can develop them and add the pictures to your record book."

"The flag!" Horace ordered.

Nolan picked it off the ground and held it firmly. Four feet above his head, the flag was clearly visible. It waved steadfast in drafts of hot air that blew toward them from the furnaces. His hand began to ache from gripping it so tightly in fear of what would happen when a Dregling caught sight of the rose emblem.

Within a few feet of the furnaces, Servan stopped and turned to Adwen. He embraced him, kissed him on the cheek, and let him go. Adwen walked back, wiping tears from his eyes, leaving his Prince and dear friend standing alone.

"What is he doing all by himself?" said Kate.

Nolan took a step forward.

"Steady," Feargus said, catching Nolan by the arm and pulling him back. "Keep that flag raised."

"They'll kill him," said Nolan.

Still with no Dreglings in sight, Prince Servan spoke loudly through the still air. "I come in the name of the King and Queen of the true Kingdom!" His voice echoed off the walls of the Gorge.

There was no response. Then a light appeared in the tower, and then another, and another. Several Dreglings in red uniforms came out onto the terraces with torches and squinted, befuddled. Other Dreglings emerged from the caves with torches in one hand and poles ready for battle in the other. The torches lit up the entire Gorge. In the next moment, at the very top of the tower in the shrine, there in a long dark robe and sparkling crown stood Grod Vurmis. The Dreglings on the cliffs rapped their poles against the walls repeatedly as one chorus, creating a deafening clatter.

Vurmis raised his hand, and the clatter stopped. Then there was the sound of marching coming up the valley behind them. Servan's troops looked back, hoping to see more Kingdom troops approaching as reinforcement. But what they saw was a company of fifty Dreglings led by red-uniformed officers. They spread across the entrance to the Gorge and stopped, blocking any way of escape. Servan and his troops were trapped.

Vurmis spoke, his voice bellowing across the Gorge. "Who is this dog who dares address me with messages from the King?"

"I come in the name of Athar and Sapienta to take our people home and take this tower down," said Servan loud enough for all to hear.

The Dreglings murmured. Finally Vurmis answered, "Who is the messenger boy who carries these demands?"

"I am Servan, Son of King Athar and Queen Sapienta."

Vurmis paused. "If you really are Prince Servan, tell me the name of the wife of one Bowman of Gulls Landing on the sea!"

As he said this, Vurmis pulled a woman toward him who wore strings of sparkling stones around her neck and a sleek dark robe and crown. Adwen gasped, recognizing his mother immediately, and raced back toward the tower. Servan raised his hand in a signal for him to stop.

"Her name is Kyla," Servan answered, "one of the many you have deceived. I demand her release along with the rest of my people you are holding here and in the towns and villages throughout the Kingdom."

"You demand?" There was a long roar of laughter from Vurmis. "This woman *was* Kyla, wife of a simple boat builder! She is now Kana, wife of Vurmis and queen of my kingdom. Unless you come with a ransom to buy her back, you will not have her. But such a jewel will exact a heavy price. What have you?"

There was silence.

"You cannot possibly be thinking of an attack with that pitiful excuse of an army you have there," Vurmis yelled, pointing to the top of the hill where Kate and the others stood. "Pitiful and thoughtless of you to take them with you to your death!" Then he swept his hand in a wide circle over the entire Gorge. "These are my loyal subjects, who have betrayed you and come home to me."

The Dreglings watched in silent disbelief at the presence of Prince Servan, alone without an army, hurling demands at their powerful master.

Suddenly, at the top of the shrine a third figure joined Vurmis and Kayla—a boy. Vurmis grabbed the boy around the neck with one arm and yelled, "Your forces are as weak and foolish as this small boy we pulled from your camp!"

Kate screamed, "Gavin!"

"He too has betrayed you, and today he has become my son." His vile, monstrous laugh rumbled through the Great Gorge.

When Gavin saw the flag in Nolan's hand, he began jumping and screaming with his fist in the air. The Dreglings still did not move, waiting for orders from their master.

Vurmis's laughter was cut short as he leaned forward, looking intently. "Is that our Feargus of Downfield?"

Feargus shouted, "It is Feargus of the true Kingdom, Friend of Servan."

Vurmis flew into a rage, his robe flying behind him as he paced in his shrine. Kayla and Gavin stumbled as he pushed them aside.

Servan spoke boldly. "Today your empire will end, Grod Vurmis. This tower will crumble, your furnaces will be choked, and your pools of poison will dry up. The people will return to their homes, to the land of their ancestors, the Ancients, the land will be healed, and the Kingdom will be ours forever."

Vurmis shouted a command that shook the Gorge. Immediately, two large doors at the base of the tower swung open. Three Dregling priests ran out in red uniforms. They dashed toward Servan, grabbed him, and shackled his hands.

"We have to go to him!" Kate yelled.

"We wait for Adwen's command," Horace said firmly.

Hewn in the rock floor of the Gorge was a square pit about ten feet across and four feet deep. They pushed Servan into the pit and fastened his shackles to iron rings at the ends of two chains that were anchored to opposite walls. He stood with his arms outstretched, the top half of his body visible above the hole. Kate's breath caught in her throat. The pit was the same one in her dream.

Servan scanned the cliffs and the tower, gazing at each of his onlookers with compassion. He suddenly grew thinner and his face younger, like that of a sixteen-year-old boy. Loud wailing broke out from the Dreglings, some exclaiming, "Servan!" as if they finally recognized him as the same young man who had lived among them years ago. Amidst the wailing were also shouts of protest from Dreglings knowing what Vurmis was about to do.

There was movement in the doorway at the base of the tower. Three moorhounds emerged, snarling and straining forward on leashes held by Dreglings. Analyse had to cover her eyes as Josephine held her tight.

The Dreglings holding the moorhounds at the edge of the pit looked up to the shrine. Vurmis held out his fist briefly and then turned his thumb down. The Dreglings released the hounds. They bound into the pit and were on Servan in an instant, ripping his clothes and burying their fangs into his arms and legs and neck. Chains clattered. The hounds dripped with blood as they pulled against one another, tearing at Servan and fighting for his body. Servan cried in agony while his audience watched in horror at the unspeakable, deadly act before them.

Kate screamed for it to stop. Finally everything went silent. Servan's body hung limp in his chains. He was dead.

The Dreglings called back the moorhounds, which slunk methodically into the tower. Then two Dreglings lifted Servan's body out of the pit and carried him to the opened doors of the furnace. Kate had to look away as they threw his body inside, and the iron doors clanged shut.

Kate, Analyse, and Nolan cried in disbelief. All the pride they felt on this mission, all the hope they had for a better Kingdom, all the faith they had in Servan—all of it faded like the sun behind a dark cloud. What they could never believe, or ever dream of in their worst nightmares, they had seen with their own eyes. Vurmis had killed their Prince.

The silence among Servan's forces and Dreglings alike was deafening. The reaction of the onlookers was fear, sadness, and shame mixed in the large caldron of the Great Gorge. Vurmis's bellow broke the silence.

"Take those as well!" He pointed to the hill where Servan's troops stood around the Kingdom flag.

But none of his subjects moved.

Adwen's voice rose loud and clear, echoing through the Gorge. "Free!" He shouted it again to the cliffs. "Free!" And again to the tower, "Free!" And once more to the Dregling troops blocking the way out of the Gorge.

There was a growing murmur among the Dreglings until a chant began, very low at first. "Free . . . free . . . free . . . free!" They looked up at Vurmis, their chants growing louder, while Vurmis tried in vain to shout over them.

In the next instant, a loud cheer went up from the great company of the disappearing and the disappeared. Dreglings raced from the tower. They were not coming after Servan's troops but dashing from Vurmis's clutches. Some took off across the suspension bridges to the rim of the Gorge. Vurmis's guards hacked through the ropes holding the bridge to stop them from leaving but not before several made it successfully across. Others fell to their deaths as the ropes broke away.

Three or four Dreglings climbed to the roof of the furnaces with Feargus among them. They took large wet wads of cloth and rammed them into the smoke stacks, plugging them so that only a wisp of the acrid fumes rose from the pipes.

The Dreglings running from the tower increased in number to a steady stream. It was chaos. Vurmis's faithful guards tried to hold back the flow, but they were outnumbered and easily overtaken. Those that could find horses rode away quickly. Others ran on foot. Those blocking the entrance of Gorge, when they saw what was happening, dropped everything and ran back down the valley.

Vurmis's priests scuttled aimlessly back and forth along the terraces, with Vurmis angrily barking out orders. "Stop them! Throw them into the pools! Kill them before they escape!"

Vurmis' commands fell unheeded against the stone walls. Then Adwen's voice rose above the escaping masses. "Return down the valley! Everyone! Return!"

Servan's faithful troops mounted their horses and rode quickly out of the Gorge, joining an increasing flow of Dreglings escaping on foot. Kate glanced back. Her heart broke as she saw Servan's riderless grey dun, still waiting obediently for its master to return. Its dark eyes looked sad, as if it knew the humble, courageous Prince would not be coming back.

Adwen called for his mother as he rode back and forth among the hundreds of people. He reached down and pulled someone up out of the crowd onto his horse. It was his mother Kyla. She was safe.

At the same time, Kate looked frantically through the crowd for her brother as people continued to rush by, but she did not see him anywhere. She called for him, fearing the worst. Josephine rode up beside her. "Come," she said, "we cannot stay. It's too dangerous. We'll find him in the crowd." Kate protested, but Josephine took hold of the bridle of Kate's horse and led her quickly out of the Gorge.

Chapter 22

On the Way Home

They turned to look back. The tower was a mile behind. Those who wanted to leave were out of harm's way, and those that chose to stay with Vurmis were probably feeling his wrath. It appeared the furnaces had stopped spewing their putrid smoke.

Horace smiled for the first time since the mission began. "Those Dreglings still have their wits about them," he said. "They've plugged up those furnaces so tight the pressure's been buildin' and she's gettin' ready to blow."

No sooner had Horace finished his thought than there was a thunderous explosion, followed by a second, that shook the ground so fiercely it made the horses rear. The blast echoed and re-echoed from the Gorge. A huge cloud of smoke rose into the air. It was the last cloud the furnaces would ever spew.

Vurmis's tower was shrouded from view but reappeared when the smoke cleared. Then it happened. They felt rumbling they thought was an earthquake. Large stones, just a few at first, were breaking from the tower and tumbling to the ground. More stones broke loose and fell, picking up momentum until the whole tower was falling in a great avalanche as if in slow motion. Vurmis and his shrine tipped from his high perch and crashed to the floor of the Gorge.

Kate screamed. "Gavin is in there!"

Within a brief minute there was nothing left of the tower but a large pile of rubble, and somewhere beneath it lay Grod Vurmis and his remaining faithful slaves.

Kate, Nolan, Analyse, and Horace stayed behind to help the stragglers while the others kept moving. They turned when they heard a horse galloping toward them from the tower. It was Feargus. With him was a second rider with two small arms wrapped around his midsection, laughing and yelling, "Yee haw! Faster! Come on, Feargus!" A ten-year-old boy's delighted face peeked around from behind Feargus. Kate put her hands to her face and peeked between her fingers to see if it really was her brother.

"Gavin!" she screamed.

"Do you want to ride with your sister?" Feargus asked his passenger.

"No way, she could never ride that fast!"

Feargus pulled up to a stop beside the others.

"Well, glad to see you again, too," Kate told Gavin, greatly relieved he had made it out alive. Kate did not ask him about his capture. There would be plenty of time to get the whole story.

As they continued to the Valley of Farms, above their heads flew a long steady stream of crows down the valley, cawing wildly. Somewhere among their flapping black wings there was a flash of white. Kate and Analyse whooped and waved as Corvus passed.

When they arrived at base camp, the faithful troops took a long rest. The Dreglings, who were actually no longer Dreglings now that they were free, continued on. They were happy to go back to their homes but nervous about the uncertainties that lay ahead. Others would continue to the palace.

The day was long with events too staggering to comprehend. The mood in camp was both elation and somberness. They had rescued Gavin, Kyla was going home, and the Kingdom of What Is was freed from the tyranny of an evil monster. Grod Vurmis was dead.

But at what horrible cost? Their beloved Servan was also dead. They would never again see his courageous figure riding high in his saddle at the front of the troops, waving them on. They would never again hear his kind, tender voice. Kate wondered what would become of the future of the Kingdom.

Grover was still recovering from the mauling of the moorhounds, but he joined them at base camp. Kate cried as she recounted the events of the day to him.

Finally she said, "I don't want to remember how he died. But he said I have to remember everything and *record* it. It's the worst job ever. It's recorded on my brain, and I'll never get it out of my head. Why do I have to put it down on paper? It's not right!"

Grover spoke. "Maybe that's what he wanted. Not just for you but for everyone else who reads about it—to remember this."

"But I just don't get it."

"Neither do I. But could you think of a better way . . . to stop Vurmis and the Plague? Imagine, Servan won the hearts and souls of all those Dreglings today. And that's just a start. Once the story gets out, there will be even more. That was worth it to him."

Nolan, who had been keeping his thoughts to himself, finally said, "Was this the King's secret plan? It's just dumb. All they had to do was ask me, and I would've gone right in as a spy and pretended to be a Dregling, and when I got close to Vurmis, I could've cut his throat."

"No you wouldn't have," Gavin piped up. "You would've never got close to Vurmis without his say so. You'd have to get past his guards. And he had those dogs guarding every passage, and man they are vicious. Only maybe three Dreglings knew how to handle them."

Grover asked Nolan, "Do you think the Dreglings would have followed you out of the Gorge after you'd done all that the same way they ran out of there after Servan got killed?"

Nolan didn't have an answer. Few people had answers, just lots of questions. They stared into the fire as the sun disappeared behind the mountains.

"He knew," Adwen said. "He knew if he gave the Dreglings a chance, and they could see him, and how far he was willing to go for them . . . they would see the difference between Vurmis and real love." Adwen put another piece of wood on the fire. "I'll forever love him."

Kate sat up in a moment of clarity. "Guys, this is the deep sorrow and great happiness. Aster—she said it was a prophesy. It was foretold."

Everyone sat for several minutes going over the day's events in their heads.

Then Adwen stood, walked over to Gavin, and sat down. He pointed to several spots on Gavin's neck and hands where his flesh had begun to disintegrate. He was starting to vanish.

"They must have really got to you back there," Adwen said softly.

The rest looked more closely at Gavin's marks and pulled back, repulsed. The marks on his hand were holes that went completely through to the other side.

"You need to tell what happened," Adwen said.

Gavin hesitated sheepishly and told them what occurred the night he was captured by the Dreglings.

"They seemed like good guys," he said. "They called a friend over with a cart who could carry the water to camp for us, and I said, sure. I called for Nolan to wait up, but he didn't hear me. Then I saw the man with the cart, his hands were disappeared, and I knew they were Dreglings. But it was too late, I couldn't run."

Gavin told them how Vurmis gave him a deluxe room in the tower with a luxury bath and personal room service and how hungry he was. They gave him a huge meal and he didn't have to eat the things he didn't feel like eating and could have all the plum trifle he wanted. And he told them how guilty he felt after eating it. "Anyway, the trifle wasn't near as good as the King and Queen's."

Gavin continued, "Vurmis did this special ceremony for me and adopted me as his son. That made me sick to my stomach, and I started thinking about how I could escape." He glanced at Kate, who was wiping tears from her eyes. "When Vurmis killed Servan, they stopped listening to him, and he got really mad and started yelling, and that's when I slipped past the guards and just ran."

As Gavin was telling his story, the openings in the flesh of his neck and hands started to fill in so that only patches like scars were left. When he'd finished, he laid his head on Adwen's shoulder and fell asleep.

Kate had not put anything in the record book about the day's events. But now she followed through with Servan's wishes, including Gavin's story, and asked Analyse to help her with some of the details. It would all be put in writing so the people would know, and the libraries of the Kingdom would grow with the stories of that day.

Kate, Analyse, Gavin, and Nolan sat at the fire long after the others had retired to their tents. Kate wondered what would happen to the Dreglings who went home. Would their families recognize them? Would Bowman take Kayla back? And something else came to mind.

"Now that the Prince is gone, there is no heir to the throne," she said, almost afraid to say the words.

Josephine sat down between Kate and Gavin and held them in her large arms. "The King and Queen rule the whole Kingdom now," she said. "Don't worry." She rocked them forward and back and hummed a tune. Her humming gave way to words in the old language, unintelligible but beautiful and hopeful. Kate bathed in it and did not want this comfort to ever end.

Horace brought them sleeping mats and blankets. They stretched out on them by the fire, huddled together, Josephine in the middle of them.

Kate looked up into the darkening sky. She could see the stars and milky way more brightly than she had ever seen them. She thought of Grover and Aster's house with the domed starry ceiling and how happy Aster would be to see this. Maybe she was watching it right now.

When they reached the palace the next day, the docks and the road up to the palace were crowed with many who had come from the Gorge and had nowhere else to turn. Several ships were being loaded with supplies for the villages on the coast, the same villages the girls had discovered on Vurmis's cave maps. Their scouting trip to the caves had paid off. These villages were in areas Vurmis had captured but were now free. They would be bringing them the good news of Vurmis's end.

The young members of Servan's special forces were ready for a good bath and some rest. The palace, however, was not the tranquil paradise they had left four days prior. Former Dreglings crowded the grounds looking for relief. From around the palace, there was a chorus of loud wailing mixed with shouts of elation. A grand restoration was underway. The air carried the smell of burnt flesh mixed with other more pleasant aromas as Shadows regained their true selves. The popping and crackling of flesh and bones materializing and coming together could be heard everywhere. Shadows were slowly fading and whole persons appearing in their place. The palace was in chaos, a wonderful chaos.

Rest for the troops would have to wait. There was work to be done. Baths and food were in high demand. Rooms were scarce and tents had to be set up for the overflow. Queen Sapienta greeted the young warriors with big hugs and quickly handed them some bedding.

"Those tents along the wall there, those people need blankets," she instructed. "When you're done with that, you can go to the dining room." Their faces brightened, until the Queen added, "Ask them what they need help with there—cooking, cleaning, serving." Then she turned to attend to someone looking for a place to lie down for the night.

Later, as the sun was setting, King Athar pulled the four young troops aside. He handed them bowls of chicken dumpling soup with cooked carrots and steaming fresh bread. He had heard several accounts of the mission but wanted to hear the story from their view also. Between bites, they recounted the events as Athar listened intently.

Finally, Kate handed the King the record book with her written account.

"I wrote down everything I could remember, with some help," she said.

King Athar held the book with gratitude and respect, then kissed it. He kissed Kate on the forehead and thanked her.

Nolan handed Athar the royal flag, but the King said Nolan should keep it. "Put it up at the front of your house, and when people ask what it's about, you can tell them your story."

There were tears in the King's eyes as he put his arms around each of them. It was clear he was wounded deeply by the loss of his son. But the King also knew that the mission had gone exactly as planned. Kate was awestruck by how the King endured these two plain but incomprehensible facts at once.

"The mission is accomplished," the King said. "But this is only the beginning."

Kate was puzzled. Were they not finished?

"You need to go back to your parents," Athar said. "They'll have missed you, and I'm sure they'll want to hear what you've been up to."

The King had a thought. "I would like to rename your town. Let me see . . . " He cleared his throat and stood tall, as a King before his many subjects, a twinkle in his eye. "I hereby decree your town, from this time forward, shall no longer be called Shall Be but Shall Be Free."

They joined with the King as he laughed with deep satisfaction.

"Shelby Free!" Gavin shouted, thrusting his fist in the air.

They were given the rooms they'd had before the mission. Kate opened her journal. She'd been so consumed with keeping a record for the King she hadn't written anything in her own notebook. But she had no sooner thought of something to put down than her pencil dropped from her hand, and she was fast asleep sitting up in bed.

She woke early the next morning to the sound of a horn honking impatiently and thought she was home again with someone waiting in a car to pick her up. She looked out to see a flock of geese in the courtyard, calling eagerly.

"Time to go!" said one, pecking at her window. "Special flight, summoned by the King!"

Kate ran to wake up Analyse, Gavin, and Nolan.

"Our ride's here, come on!"

Rubbing sleep from their eyes, they followed Kate out to their waiting flight crew. Four geese strapped on the travelers' backpacks, and Kate repeated the instructions for proper goose flight for the benefit of the less experienced passengers.

"Put your chest on the back of your front goose, like this," she demonstrated, "and your feet on the back of your rear goose, like this. Now hang on without strangling your goose and enjoy the ride!"

In a chorus of honking that must have woken the entire palace, Kate, Analyse, and Gavin lifted off, with Nolan still on the ground. Lifting him required summoning a third goose, but soon he was up and following them.

The geese wheeled back over the castle. It glistened in the rising sun—majestic, broken, and beautiful. Kate felt a deep affection for the palace and a melancholy at saying good-bye. She had been changed in this place. They had all changed.

Nolan's geese struggled to keep up and maintain a straight course. His gangly arms and legs made a smooth flight problematic. The others looked back, concerned, and saw legs flopping back and forth as he hung on, his flag fluttering behind him like a loose tail fin.

"Don't worry, we're fine! We don't mind zigzag lines!" the geese called.

The miles disappeared quickly behind them, which felt strange after having traveled on foot and horseback for so long. What adventures they would have missed going by goose! Their long trek had given them a love of the land they would never lose.

There was a chill in the air, and as they flew, they were suddenly enveloped in a cloud that obscured their view. Kate felt a moment of panicked helplessness, expecting to be overcome by the horrid odor again. All she could do was hang on and trust the geese to navigate through it. What she smelled, however, was not the odor of the Plague but the musky scent of autumn in the cool, moist clouds.

As they broke through the cloud, they noticed more signs of change. The woods displayed shades of yellow and orange and red, laid out like a Thanksgiving dinner table. It was as though the land of What Is had been held hostage for years and was suddenly released. And now she had found her clothes of forgotten colors and was changing with a flamboyant urgency. She was making up for lost time.

Plum season was finally over, to the satisfaction of many. People had been starting to grumble a new proverb, "Plums are delicious but too many are malicious." But now people could enjoy the foods of fall—grapes, grouse, potatoes, and pumpkins. And the snows would come eventually, too, so the land could rest, as Sapienta said, with new life lying in wait.

In minutes, Singing Meadow appeared and ahead lay Budsley Pond.

The lead goose called, "Must drop you off without hesitation or elaboration, and hightail it to nether regions. Our reasons are in the season. Excuse if we insist, it's a call we can't resist." They had long overstayed their welcome in the north, and they were looking forward to some mucky southern swamps. With that final declaration, the flock honked their boisterous affirmation and glided downward toward Budsley Pond.

The geese with the backpacks dropped their luggage on the bank of the pond.

"Ready for landing!" cried the geese.

The goose transport glided to four feet above the water. The rear goose in each pair pulled back with a frantic flapping while the lead goose took a quick left turn, shaking their passengers loose and sending them tumbling into the pond, arms and legs flailing. The beavers dove for cover as the passengers hit the water with four large splashes. Water sprayed everywhere.

The Four Fugitives whooped wildly. "Awesome! Do it again!"

Dripping on the bank of the pond, they watched as the geese diminished to flickering dots on the southern horizon.

The thought of leaving What Is settled in their stomachs like stale fries. They didn't want to go back home. Where *was* home? Didn't they belong here more than in Shelby? They felt more alive than ever here. How could they go back to the lifeless "normal" of Shelby?

But the King was right—their parents deserved an explanation. They should hear their story. Though Kate would go back to a house without Dad, she could face it now, she thought. The dark cloud she had battled was gone.

"Are we telling anyone?" Analyse asked. "My parents would lock me up and throw away the key if I tried to explain any of this."

Kate said, "Just telling them might not be enough. People need to see it for themselves. 'Shelby shall be free' so maybe they'll get it if they actually see it."

"Hey, look," said Analyse. "Nolan, show us your ears."

Nolan pulled back his hair. His ears were completely whole without any lines or ridges. The scars on Gavin's hands and neck were also gone. Analyse and Kate looked at each other. Their lips were smooth again without cracks. They looked out over the pond. The beavers were back, more than before, constructing a second lodge, and kingfishers and swallows were darting over the water. The pond showed no signs of the Plague.

Before ducking through Wild Rose Passage, the four turned one last time, but even as they did, they knew this would not be their last good-bye.

Chapter 23

Lights in the Sky

When Kate and Analyse emerged on the Shelby side, Nolan and Gavin were not with them. They called back through the rose hedge. Perhaps the boys hadn't followed and run off. The girls ducked back through the bushes, and there they were.

"Why didn't you come out with us?" Kate said.

"Why didn't *you* come out?" Nolan said. "We were right there at the park waiting, and then we came back in here to look for you."

"Wait," said Analyse, "what time does your watch say, Nolan?"

It had stopped at 1:24. She pushed up her glasses and gave a deep sigh. She showed them her watch, which had stopped at 10:55.

"Okay, we have a time problem here," Analyse explained. "Kate and I came in here after hanging out in the park Saturday morning with Nolan, right? You two came here a couple hours later in the afternoon, obviously."

"Huh?" said Gavin.

"That means out there in Shelby we're stuck in different times. And we'll stay stuck if we all leave here at once because it will be Saturday morning for me and Kate and Saturday afternoon for you guys, and we'll be forever living two hours apart!"

Gavin said, "Cool!"

"True, we could think about it as a positive," Analyse mused. "Wouldn't that be nice."

"Get serious," Kate said. "It means we'd never see Gavin and Nolan again. Ever."

"Okay guys, we'll do this," Analyse said. "Kate and I will leave now, and this afternoon at precisely 1:14, the time you guys first came in, we'll come back for you. Then we'll be on the same time."

They agreed to the plan. The boys would stay in What Is, and the girls would meet them in a couple hours at Rocky Mound.

When Kate arrived home, her mom was not there. Norbert stood in the kitchen and looked up at her. Kate picked him up and gave him several long strokes. The house was so quiet she could hear the wall clock ticking. She phoned her dad. No, he had not forgotten their lunch date. He had something for her.

"At Max's Burgers?" she said. "I can be there in ten minutes."

At Max's Kate didn't touch her burger. She didn't feel the taste for it yet. Also, she was wondering how to explain things and how much to tell him.

Before she could say anything, her dad said, "I want to give you your birthday present, but first I have some good news. Maybe not everything we want, but a little bit of good news."

"What?"

"We've been talking, your mom and I, and we came to an agreement. I'll come home as often as I want, but it will be for short visits, an hour or so for now. I'll stay living in my own apartment. For now anyway, and who knows . . . "

"Whatever you've done, Dad, say you're sorry, really sorry, and Mom needs to forgive you and get over it. Just make up and come home. It's like you've disappeared." She shuddered, imagining him as a Shadow in the Kingdom of What Is.

"It will take some time," he said. He cleared his throat, leaned forward, and creased his napkin. "I have to tell you something, honey, and Gavin too. There was, uh . . . I was unfaithful to your mom . . . over a period of time . . . and that's why I had to leave."

Kate screwed up her mouth. "I figured as much. You could have just said so."

"Well . . . it was wrong. The other woman—"

"It's okay, Dad, I don't need the details. You and Mom just have to make up. If you can break up, you can make up, right?"

"I wish it were that easy. It's a journey, as they say. But time is our friend."

Kate sat up. "How about a journey out of time?"

"What do you mean?"

"Time Out Woods."

Her dad brightened. "Sure, I'd love it. A good hike would do us good. How about going to one of our favorite spots—Miner's Gulch maybe, although that's a bit far. Your mom invited me for dinner tomorrow, so I'll come early, and maybe we can visit Burton Pond or see the salmon run. They're spawning now, you know."

"This time I'm the leader," Kate said.

"Sure."

"And maybe even Mom could join us," Kate offered.

"Let's not push it, okay. We'll see."

Her dad took a wrapped box from his briefcase and gave it to Kate. "Happy birthday."

Before Kate opened it, she picked up her dad's briefcase. "I wanted to do this again," she said and put her face inside and took a deep breath.

Her dad laughed, remembering the little girl who always loved wearing his briefcase on her head.

Kate unwrapped the box and opened it. Inside was a beautifully bound journal with a leather cover.

"To record your discoveries in Time Out Woods," he said, seeing it as a brilliant idea for a gift. "The cover is removable, so you can use it for your next journal, too."

Kate laughed.

"You don't like it?" he asked.

"No, I love it." She wondered if she should show him her journal. No, he would see What Is for himself.

Kate held the gift to her chest and said confidently, "We'll be together again, Dad, one family again. I know this."

He smiled. "Together."

As they left Max's, Kate felt herself relax. She no longer carried a backpack filled with the weight of her mom and dad. She had carried it too long, and the cloud of sorrow that had been hovering around her for months was miles off now, slipping over the horizon. She was happy. She felt herself flying all the way back to Wild Rose Passage.

At 1:14 sharp, Kate and Analyse passed through the hedge. Nolan and Gavin were at their agreed meeting spot on Rocky Mound. They played the rest of the afternoon and into the evening, jumping from rock to rock, making grass whistles, and hanging out. They looked out over the grass-covered hills that had been the beginning of their quest.

"Our dad is coming here tomorrow night with Gavin and me, and maybe Mom," Kate said.

"I don't think mine will," Analyse said. "Their loss."

Kate said, "I want to be riding on the flag ship with Bowman and Kyla."

"I'd like to be at the palace right now," Analyse said, "with a book from the Royal Library."

Kate went over to Nolan and sat down. "Thanks," she said.

"Sure, for what?"

She reached into her jacket pocket. "Here's your phone back."

"Hey, when did you steal that?"

"I've had it since the palace. I wanted to see the pictures you took, but they're not on there."

"What! You are so toast if you deleted them." Nolan desperately scrolled through his picture files. "They *are* here, look."

Kate looked and shrugged. "Okay, so they are. But they won't be there when you get back to Shelby, I checked. They don't show up out there."

"What? But our evidence!"

"Hey, cool it. Listen, your evidence is right there." She put her finger on his chest.

Nolan looked down at his chest and thought.

As the light faded, the sky began filling with waves of red and green and yellow, dancing across the sky from north to south.

"The northern lights!" Nolan yelled, standing up.

They watched in amazement.

"Real Star Wars!" Nolan said almost breathless. "My first time seeing this—it's so bright."

"It means all the animals that have died are dancing," Analyse said. "It's in the native folklore."

Kate stood and mimicked the waves of light, twirling at the top of Rocky Mound, her hands waving in the air. Analyse joined in. The two of them created a northern lights choreography that involved a dancing bear and a dancing deer.

"It's like an ocean in the sky," Kate said. "The waves—they just keep coming!"

Just then a dark bird dropped out of the sky, silhouetted in the northern lights, with one white wing feather that stood out like a falling star. The bird settled down into a nook on one rock.

"Hey!" Kate said. "I thought you might show up."

"I never miss a party. And you all have arrived early!" Corvus said. He lifted his beak. "The air has a particular luster tonight—great night for a celebration. Some geese are gathering for a feeding frenzy before their trip south. The bears are raiding a patch of ripe salmon berries over in the gulley. And the beavers at the pond—they're actually doing nothing all night but sitting around and drinking mint-and-pond-water cocktails."

The sky filled with deep, rich waves of green and red, shimmering toward them from the north as though emanating directly from the palace.

Gavin broke their concentration. "Corvus?"

"Yes, my young friend."

"Where did you go after we saw you at Fisherman's Cove?"

Never one to disappoint a captive audience, Corvus told them what he and his gang had been up to. After Fisherman's Cove, they had flown further up the coast beyond Gulls Landing to a village called Windover, which Dreglings had taken control of. At Windover the crows decided to practice a little trickery of their own, he said. As Corvus began his story, the four leaned in like conspiring warriors.

"We hid back in the trees, you see, a few feet from the village, just waiting. Well, about sundown we put up a squawking like a bunch of crazy kids arguing with their parents . . . no offense to present company intended. Anyway, we had them at the first squawk. Dreglings came running into the woods to find out who was carrying on because they thought some people of the village must be trying to run away, right? So, as soon as . . . "

Corvus had to pause because he began laughing. And the harder he tried not to laugh, the harder he laughed.

"Come on, Corvus, tell the story," begged Gavin.

"So, as soon as they got close, we flew off a little further and tried our squabbling ploy again, and they followed again. We kept going, you see, until we had them so deep in the woods they didn't know where they were anymore or how to get back." Corvus started laughing again.

"And what happened?" Gavin demanded. "Corvus, stop laughing."

Corvus gasped. "Well, by this time it was dark, and we . . . we left them turning circles . . . cursing each other!"

Now Corvus laughed uncontrollably until he was crying and fell onto his back. He held his stomach, trying to catch his breath. The rest of them could not help themselves anymore and were in stitches, too.

"Anyway . . . this is the best part," he said, managing to prop himself up on one wing. "Of course, they didn't know where the heck those voices were coming from . . . and they thought the whole woods must be haunted! So they just left the village and the whole area, and victory was ours!"

Corvus finally got himself to his feet, exhausted from laughter, thanked them for bearing with him, and flexed his wings.

"This is the best I've felt for years!" he sighed. "Well, I must be getting back to my gang. We're planning a little fun and revelry. Jim and Mim have caught a couple snakes for a feast, Jules has thrown together a fruit salad from various bits discovered in your park, and we've also found a good large log full of millipedes."

Corvus stretched, waved a brief farewell, and caught a draft that lifted him swiftly into the autumn night.

It was quiet except for beavers singing at Budsley Pond. The northern lights were fading to occasional glimmers on the horizon. The moon came up full and bathed the hills in a sea of muted blue. Nolan put his jacket over Kate's shoulders, and she pulled it tightly around her against the night air. To the east, the mountain peaks had donned a shawl of fresh snow that glowed in the waning waves of green, red, and gold lights. Winter was not far away.

Acknowledgments

We never accomplish anything on our own. Each of us is surrounded by a crowd of influencers. My dad is in that crowd. He was a great storyteller. He'd draw you in with his soothing tones and wry grin, and before you knew it, you were hooked, sometimes as the subject of his story.

My two daughters have compelled me to follow in the happy tradition of storytellers. Before *The Kingdom of What Is* came to be, they constantly prodded me for the bedtime stories that planted the seed for the story you hold in your hands. I can confidently say, without them this would never have been written.

I also could not have completed this without the help of many other kids who read early drafts and portions of the novel—Lucas, Emma, Maya, Bryn, Anastasia, Ruby, Mia, Calvin, Isaac, and Isaac. Their honest, unfiltered feedback made this story better.

A big thank you to Nikki Winter, Melinda Bratt, Hillary Fuhrman, and my enthusiastic editor, Lydia Forssander-Song. Their literary insights, keen eyes, encouragement, and understanding of what kids love kept me on track. Thanks also to Leah Kostamo, who pointed me to Wipf and Stock Publishers, who in turn took a chance on my manuscript.

Thank you to the staff at Willow Cafe for keeping me going with coffee and a sunny perch from which to think and work.

Last, I sincerely thank Diane, my longsuffering wife, who put up with my many moods and my incessant pecking at this novel before I could let it go. Anyone who thinks it would be exciting to live with a writer should have a talk with her first.

CPSIA information can be obtained
at www.ICGtesting.com
Printed in the USA
LVHW050320260123
737945LV00008B/506